& Co

#7 HOME FOR THE HOLIDAYS

BASED ON THE ORIGINAL CHARACTERS CREATED BY

JIM DAVIS

PAPERCUTZ ™

NEW YORK

GARFIELD & Co

GRAPHIC NOVELS AVAILABLE FROM **PAPERCUTZ** ™

GRAPHIC NOVEL #1
"FISH TO FRY"

GRAPHIC NOVEL #2
"THE CURSE OF
THE CAT PEOPLE"

GRAPHIC NOVEL #3
"CATZILLA"

GRAPHIC NOVEL #4
"CAROLING CAPERS"

GRAPHIC NOVEL #5
"A GAME OF CAT
AND MOUSE"

GRAPHIC NOVEL #6
"MOTHER GARFIELD"

GRAPHIC NOVEL #7
"HOME FOR
THE HOLIDAYS"

COMING SOON:

GRAPHIC NOVEL #8
"SECRET AGENT X"

GARFIELD & Co 7 - HOME FOR THE HOLIDAYS
"THE GARFIELD SHOW" SERIES © 2012- DARGAUD MEDIA.
ALL RIGHTS RESERVED. © PAWS. "GARFIELD" & GARFIELD
CHARACTERS ™ & © PAWS INC.- ALL RIGHTS RESERVED.
THE GARFIELD SHOW- A DARGAUD MEDIA PRODUCTION.
IN ASSOCIATION WITH FRANCE3 WITH. THE PARTICIPATION
OF CENTRE NATIONAL DE LA CINÉMETAGRAPHIE AND THE
SUPPORT OF REGION LLE-DE-FRANCE. A SERIES DEVELOPED
BY PHILIPPE VIDAL, ROBERT REA & STEVE BALISSAT. BASED
UPON THE CHARACTERS CREATED BY JIM DAVIS. ORIGINAL
STORIES: "HOME FOR THE HOLIDAYS" WRITTEN BY JIM
DAVIS; "THE HAUNTED HOUSE" WRITTEN BY MARK EVANIER.

CEDRIC MICHIELS - COMICS ADAPTATION
JOE JOHNSON - TRANSLATIONS
JIM SALICRUP - DIALOGUE RESTORATION
JANICE CHIANG - LETTERING
ADAM GRANO - PRODUCTION
MICHAEL PETRANEK - ASSOCIATE EDITOR
JIM SALICRUP
EDITOR-IN-CHIEF

ISBN: 978-1-59707-370-7

PRINTED IN CHINA
SEPTEMBER 2012 BY O.G. PRINTING PRODUCTIONS, LTD.
UNITS 2 & 3, 5/F, LEMMI CENTRE
50 HOI YUEN ROAD
KWON TONG, KOWLOON

DISTRIBUTED BY MACMILLAN
FIRST PAPERCUTZ PRINTING

GARFIELD & Co GRAPHIC NOVELS ARE AVAILABLE AT BOOK-
SELLERS EVERYWHERE IN HARDCOVER ONLY FOR $7.99 EACH.

OR ORDER FROM US - PLEASE ADD $4.00 FOR POSTAGE AND HANDLING FOR
THE FIRST BOOK, ADD $1.00 FOR EACH ADDITIONAL BOOK. PLEASE MAKE CHECK
PAYABLE TO: NBM PUBLISHING SEND TO: PAPERCUTZ, 160 BROADWAY, SUITE
700, EAST WING, NEW YORK, NY 10038 (1-800-886-1223)

WWW.PAPERCUTZ.COM

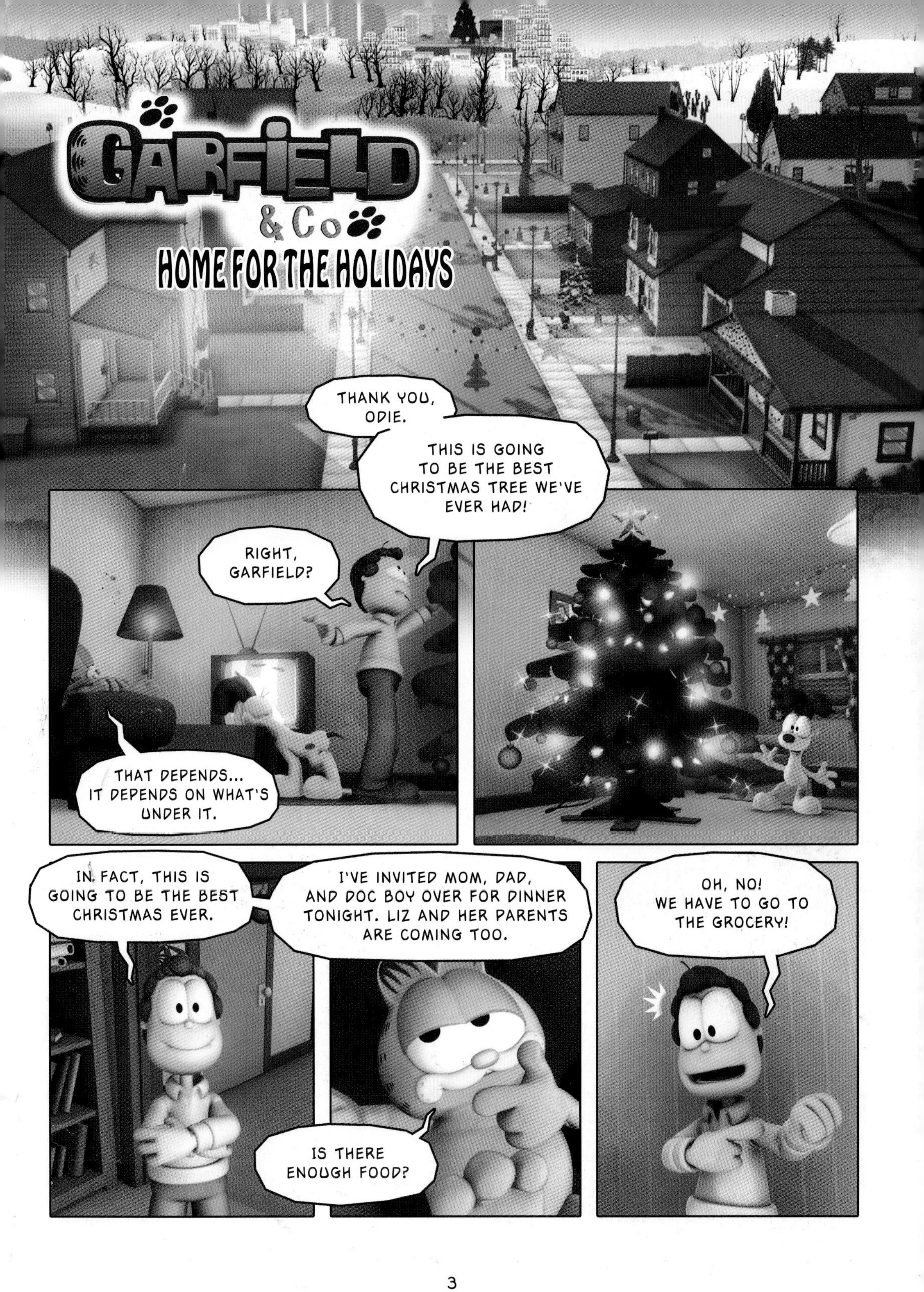

GARFIELD
& Co
HOME FOR THE HOLIDAYS
THANK YOU, ODIE.
THIS IS GOING TO BE THE BEST CHRISTMAS TREE WE'VE EVER HAD!
RIGHT, GARFIELD?
THAT DEPENDS... IT DEPENDS ON WHAT'S UNDER IT.
IN FACT, THIS IS GOING TO BE THE BEST CHRISTMAS EVER.
I'VE INVITED MOM, DAD, AND DOC BOY OVER FOR DINNER TONIGHT. LIZ AND HER PARENTS ARE COMING TOO.
IS THERE ENOUGH FOOD?
OH, NO! WE HAVE TO GO TO THE GROCERY!

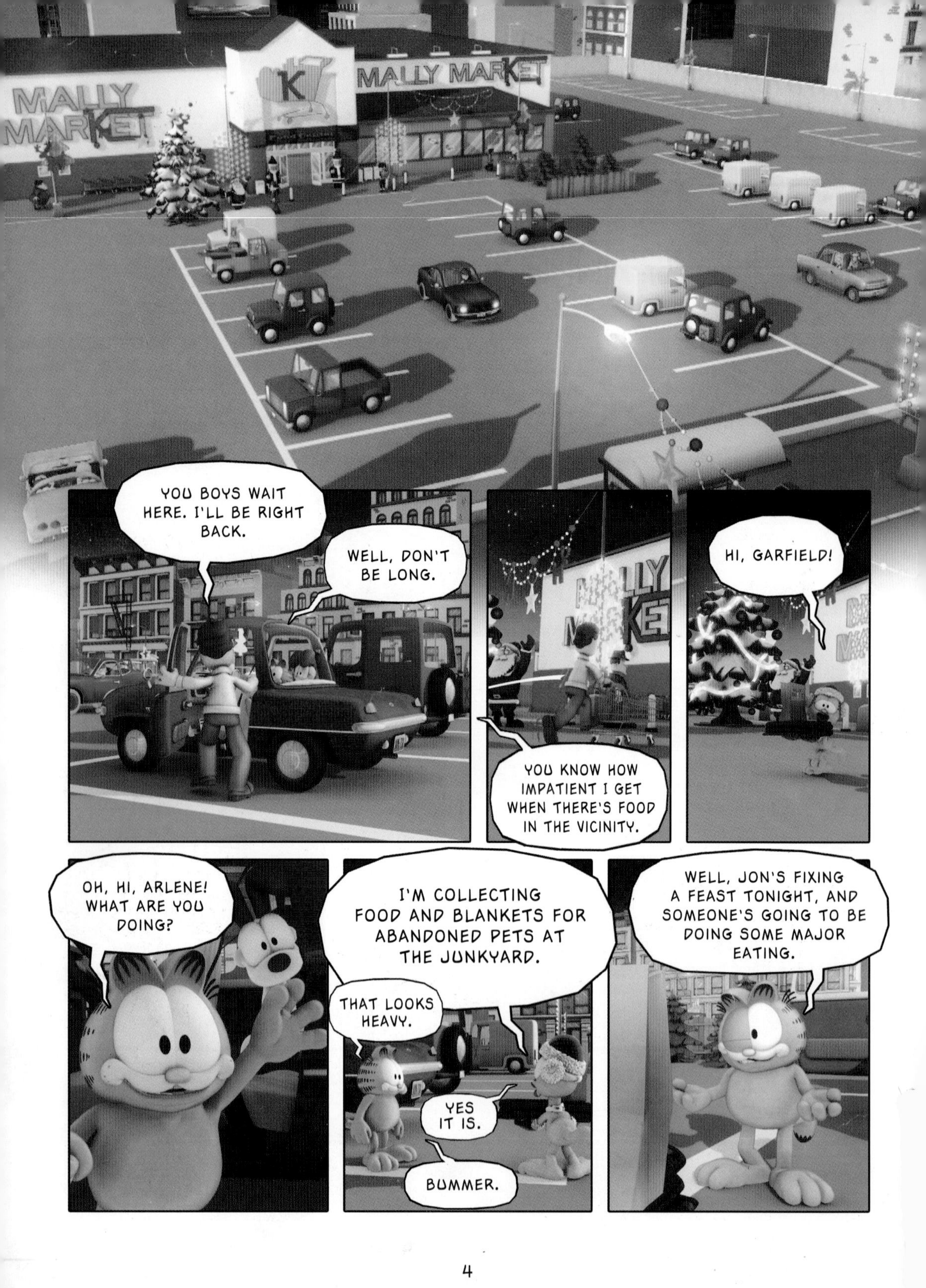

YOU BOYS WAIT HERE. I'LL BE RIGHT BACK.
WELL, DON'T BE LONG.
YOU KNOW HOW IMPATIENT I GET WHEN THERE'S FOOD IN THE VICINITY.
HI, GARFIELD!
OH, HI, ARLENE! WHAT ARE YOU DOING?
I'M COLLECTING FOOD AND BLANKETS FOR ABANDONED PETS AT THE JUNKYARD.
THAT LOOKS HEAVY.
YES IT IS.
BUMMER.
WELL, JON'S FIXING A FEAST TONIGHT, AND SOMEONE'S GOING TO BE DOING SOME MAJOR EATING.

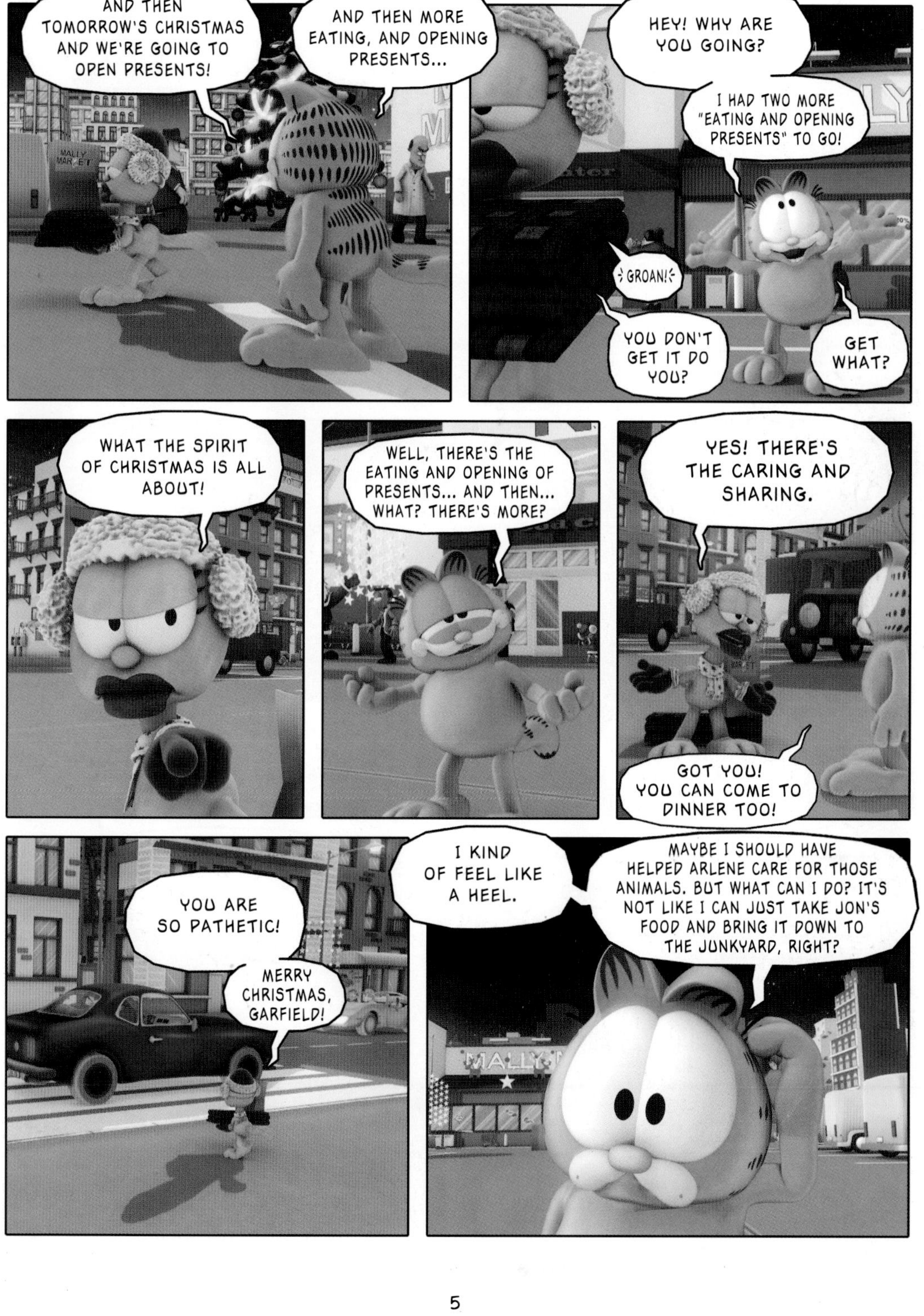
AND THEN TOMORROW'S CHRISTMAS AND WE'RE GOING TO OPEN PRESENTS!
AND THEN MORE EATING, AND OPENING PRESENTS...
HEY! WHY ARE YOU GOING?
I HAD TWO MORE "EATING AND OPENING PRESENTS" TO GO!
GROAN!
YOU DON'T GET IT DO YOU?
GET WHAT?
WHAT THE SPIRIT OF CHRISTMAS IS ALL ABOUT!
WELL, THERE'S THE EATING AND OPENING OF PRESENTS... AND THEN... WHAT? THERE'S MORE?
YES! THERE'S THE CARING AND SHARING.
GOT YOU! YOU CAN COME TO DINNER TOO!
YOU ARE SO PATHETIC!
MERRY CHRISTMAS, GARFIELD!
I KIND OF FEEL LIKE A HEEL.
MAYBE I SHOULD HAVE HELPED ARLENE CARE FOR THOSE ANIMALS. BUT WHAT CAN I DO? IT'S NOT LIKE I CAN JUST TAKE JON'S FOOD AND BRING IT DOWN TO THE JUNKYARD, RIGHT?

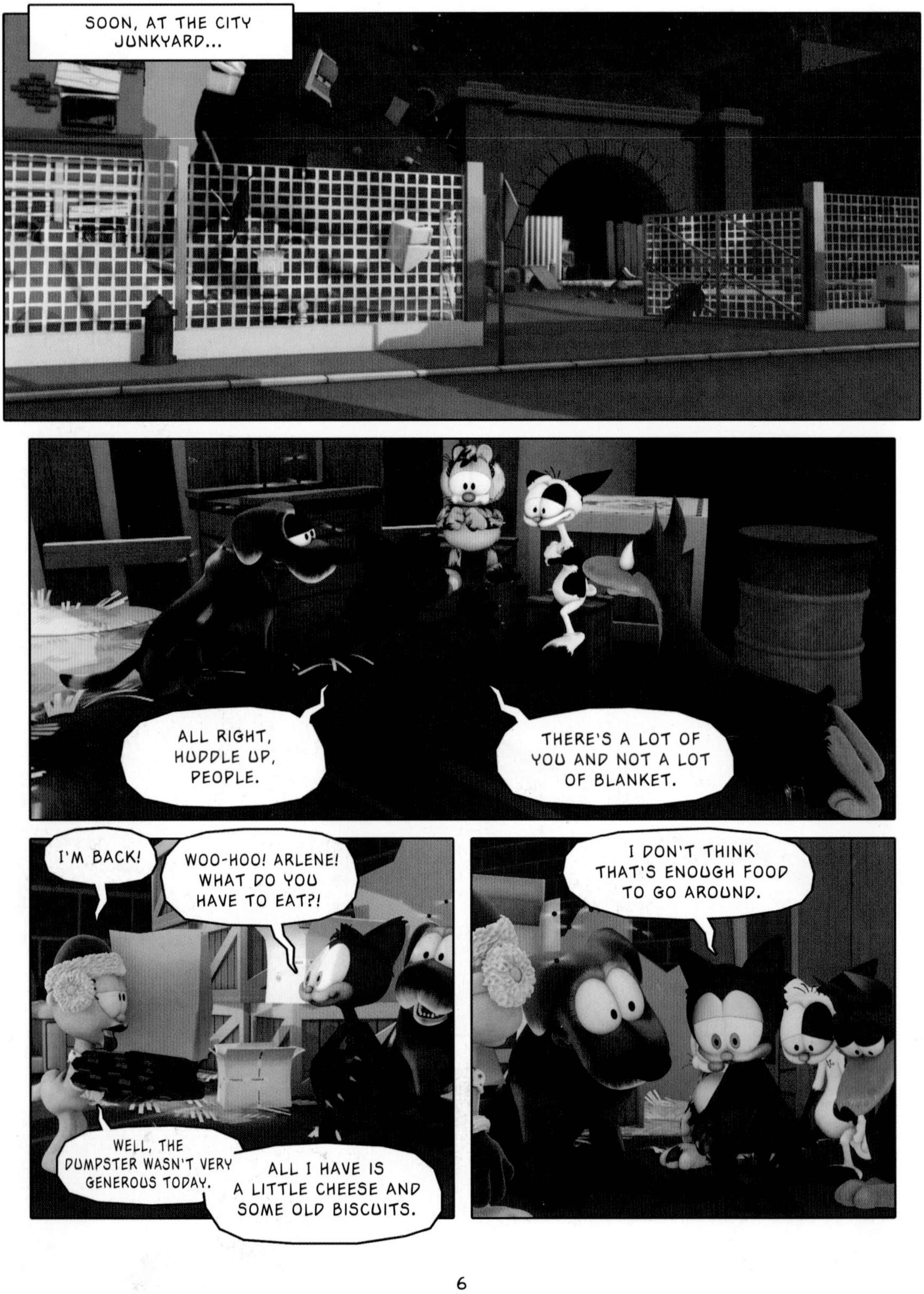
SOON, AT THE CITY JUNKYARD...
ALL RIGHT, HUDDLE UP, PEOPLE.
THERE'S A LOT OF YOU AND NOT A LOT OF BLANKET.
I'M BACK!
WOO-HOO! ARLENE! WHAT DO YOU HAVE TO EAT?!
WELL, THE DUMPSTER WASN'T VERY GENEROUS TODAY.
ALL I HAVE IS A LITTLE CHEESE AND SOME OLD BISCUITS.
I DON'T THINK THAT'S ENOUGH FOOD TO GO AROUND.

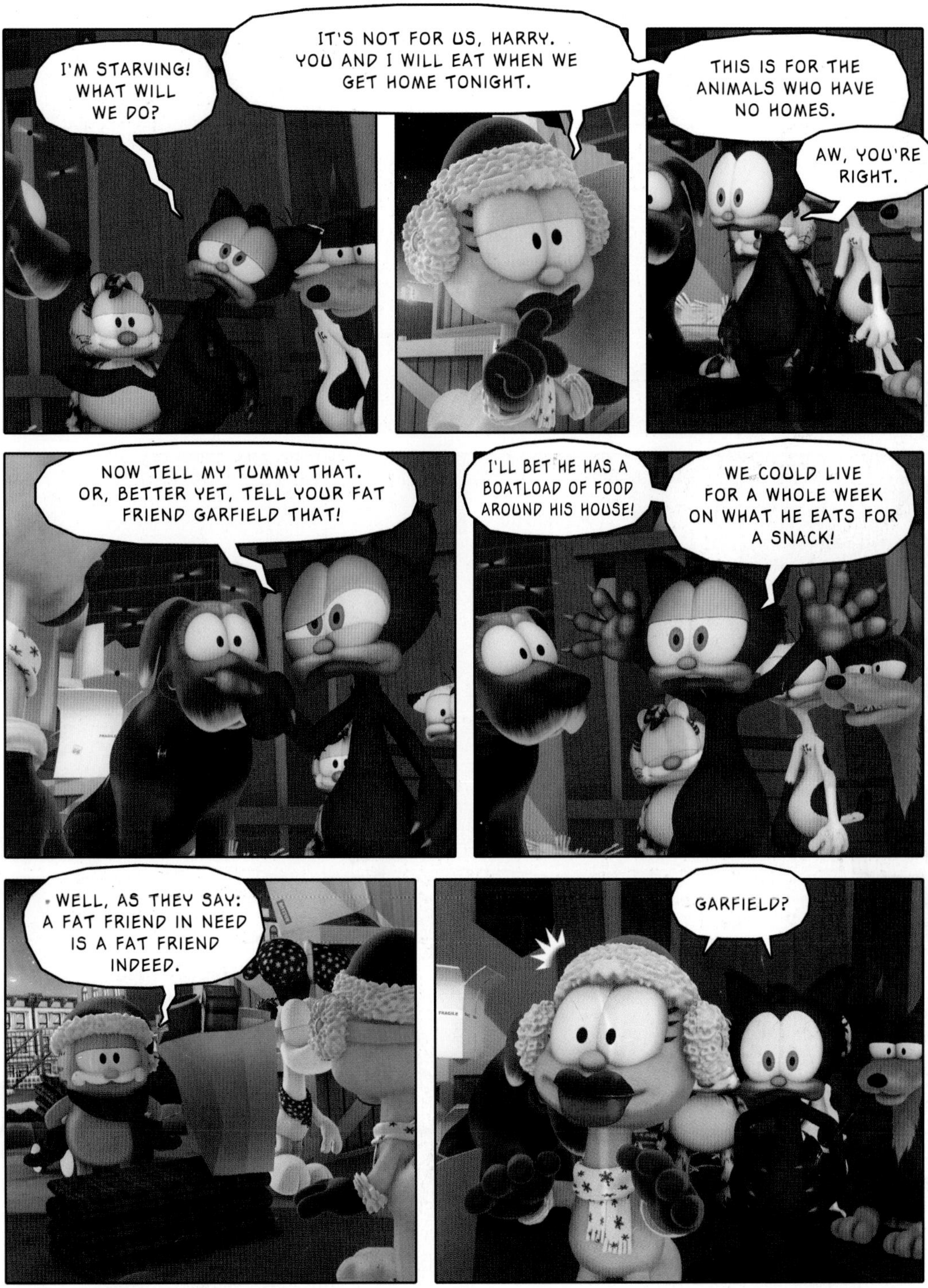
I'M STARVING! WHAT WILL WE DO?
IT'S NOT FOR US, HARRY. YOU AND I WILL EAT WHEN WE GET HOME TONIGHT.
THIS IS FOR THE ANIMALS WHO HAVE NO HOMES.
AW, YOU'RE RIGHT.
NOW TELL MY TUMMY THAT. OR, BETTER YET, TELL YOUR FAT FRIEND GARFIELD THAT!
I'LL BET HE HAS A BOATLOAD OF FOOD AROUND HIS HOUSE!
WE COULD LIVE FOR A WHOLE WEEK ON WHAT HE EATS FOR A SNACK!
WELL, AS THEY SAY: A FAT FRIEND IN NEED IS A FAT FRIEND INDEED.
GARFIELD?

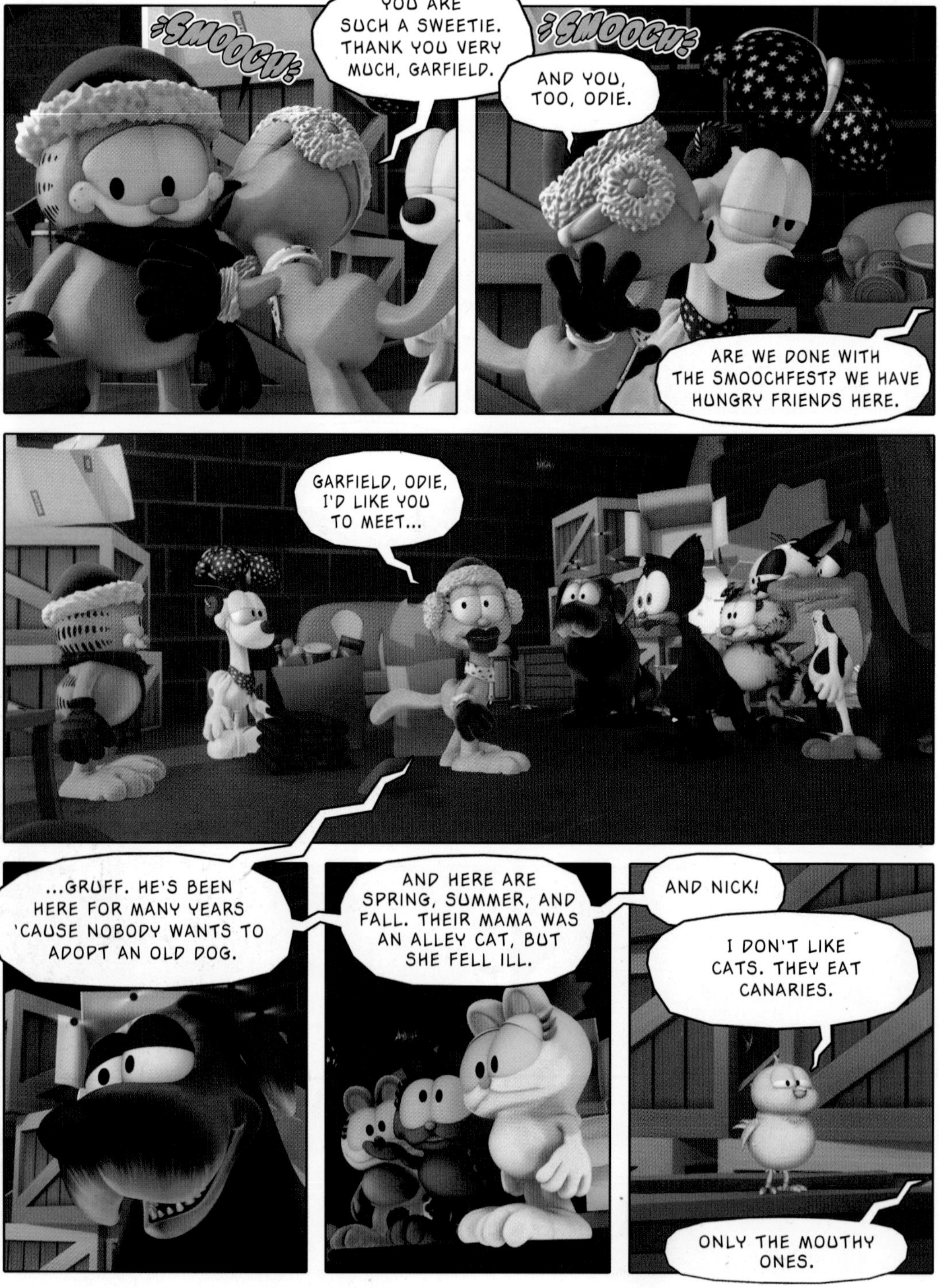
SMOOCH
YOU ARE SUCH A SWEETIE. THANK YOU VERY MUCH, GARFIELD.
SMOOCH
AND YOU, TOO, ODIE.
ARE WE DONE WITH THE SMOOCHFEST? WE HAVE HUNGRY FRIENDS HERE.
GARFIELD, ODIE, I'D LIKE YOU TO MEET...
...GRUFF. HE'S BEEN HERE FOR MANY YEARS 'CAUSE NOBODY WANTS TO ADOPT AN OLD DOG.
AND HERE ARE SPRING, SUMMER, AND FALL. THEIR MAMA WAS AN ALLEY CAT, BUT SHE FELL ILL.
AND NICK!
I DON'T LIKE CATS. THEY EAT CANARIES.
ONLY THE MOUTHY ONES.

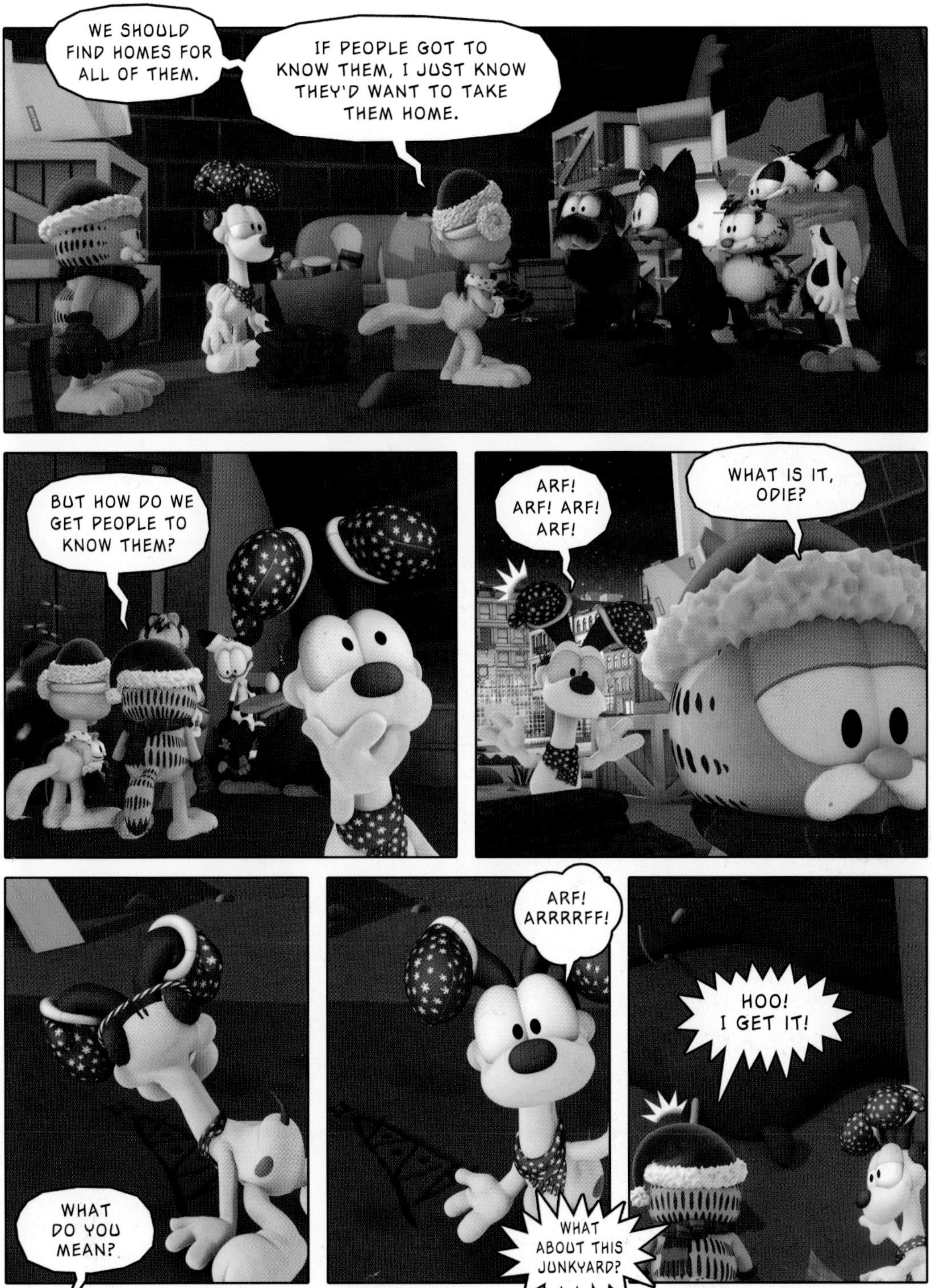
WE SHOULD FIND HOMES FOR ALL OF THEM.
IF PEOPLE GOT TO KNOW THEM, I JUST KNOW THEY'D WANT TO TAKE THEM HOME.
BUT HOW DO WE GET PEOPLE TO KNOW THEM?
ARF! ARF! ARF! ARF!
WHAT IS IT, ODIE?
WHAT DO YOU MEAN?
ARF! ARRRRFF!
WHAT ABOUT THIS JUNKYARD?
HOO! I GET IT!

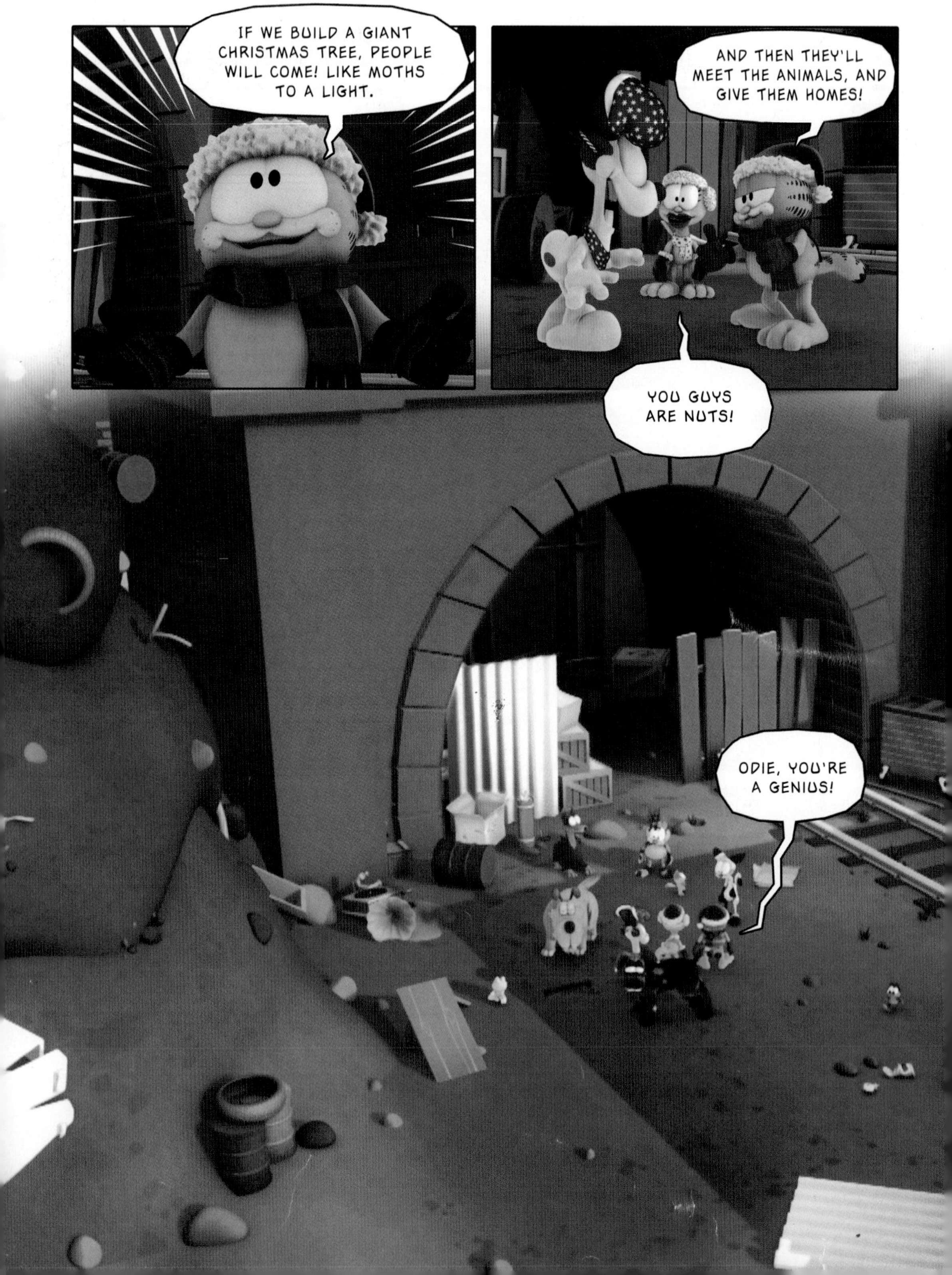
IF WE BUILD A GIANT CHRISTMAS TREE, PEOPLE WILL COME! LIKE MOTHS TO A LIGHT.
AND THEN THEY'LL MEET THE ANIMALS, AND GIVE THEM HOMES!
YOU GUYS ARE NUTS!
ODIE, YOU'RE A GENIUS!

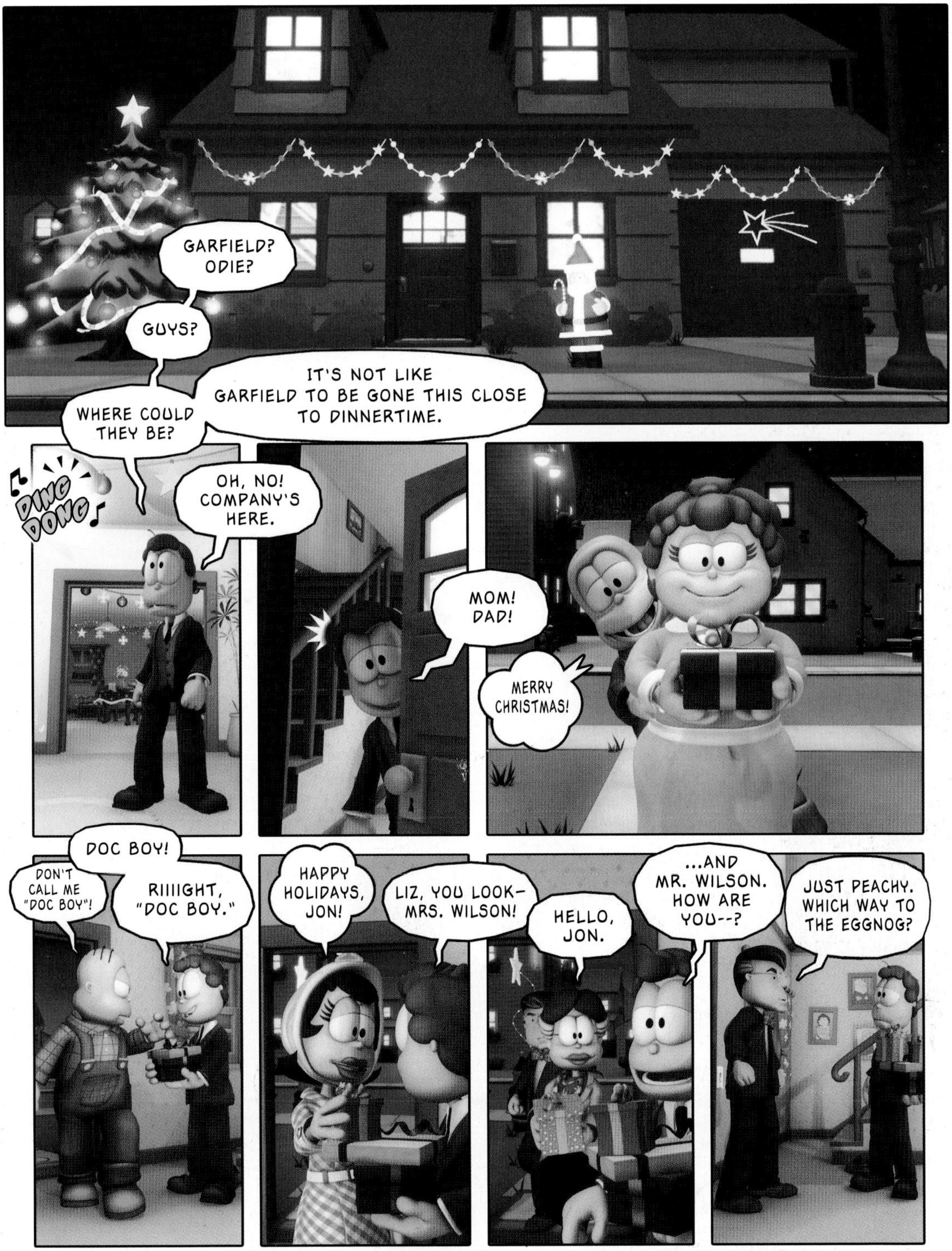
GARFIELD? ODIE?
GUYS?
WHERE COULD THEY BE?
IT'S NOT LIKE GARFIELD TO BE GONE THIS CLOSE TO DINNERTIME.
DING DONG
OH, NO! COMPANY'S HERE.
MOM! DAD!
MERRY CHRISTMAS!
DOC BOY!
DON'T CALL ME "DOC BOY"!
RIIIIGHT, "DOC BOY."
HAPPY HOLIDAYS, JON!
LIZ, YOU LOOK— MRS. WILSON!
HELLO, JON.
...AND MR. WILSON. HOW ARE YOU--?
JUST PEACHY. WHICH WAY TO THE EGGNOG?

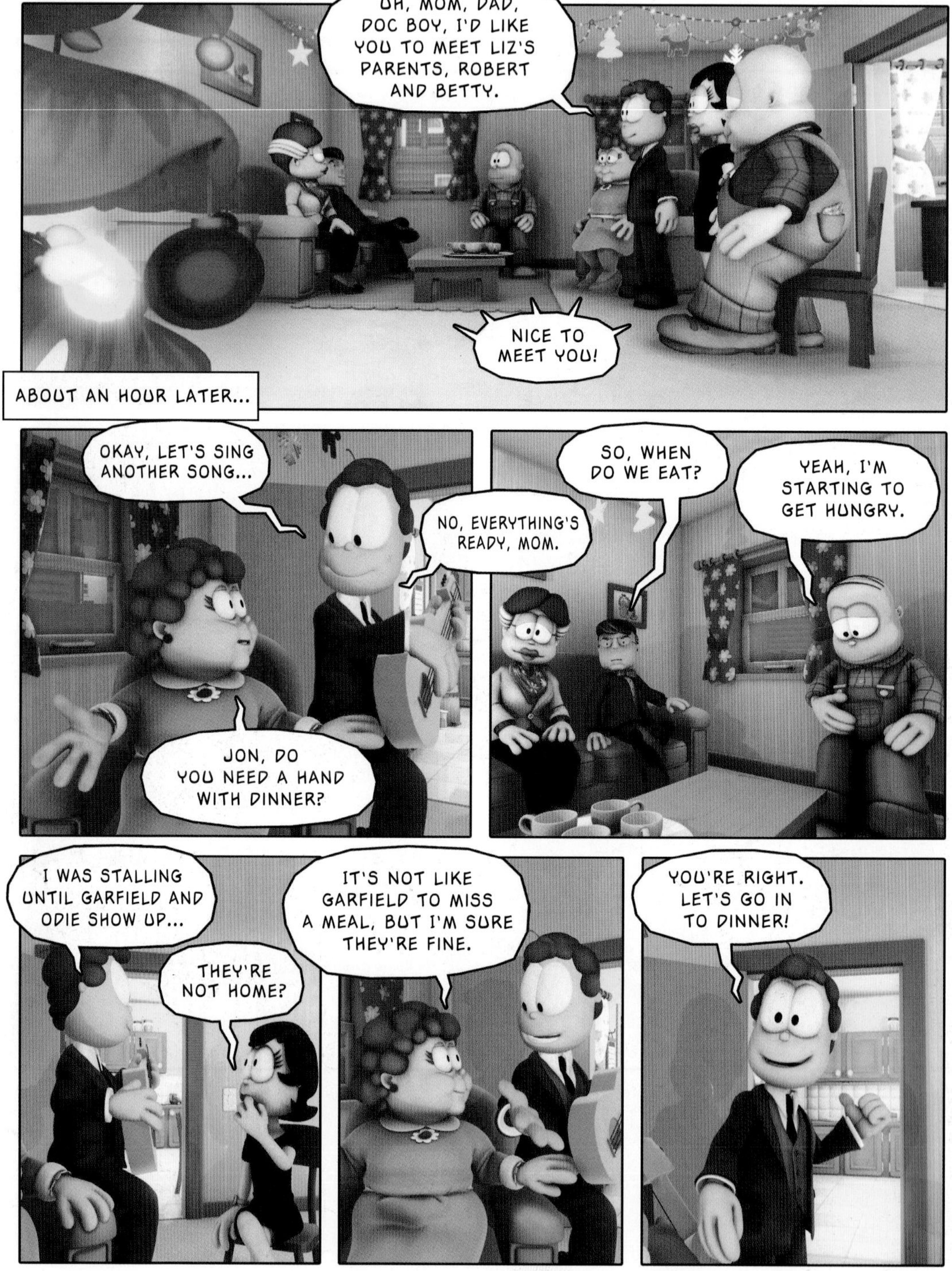
UH, MOM, DAD, DOC BOY, I'D LIKE YOU TO MEET LIZ'S PARENTS, ROBERT AND BETTY.
NICE TO MEET YOU!
ABOUT AN HOUR LATER...
OKAY, LET'S SING ANOTHER SONG...
JON, DO YOU NEED A HAND WITH DINNER?
NO, EVERYTHING'S READY, MOM.
SO, WHEN DO WE EAT?
YEAH, I'M STARTING TO GET HUNGRY.
I WAS STALLING UNTIL GARFIELD AND ODIE SHOW UP...
THEY'RE NOT HOME?
IT'S NOT LIKE GARFIELD TO MISS A MEAL, BUT I'M SURE THEY'RE FINE.
YOU'RE RIGHT. LET'S GO IN TO DINNER!

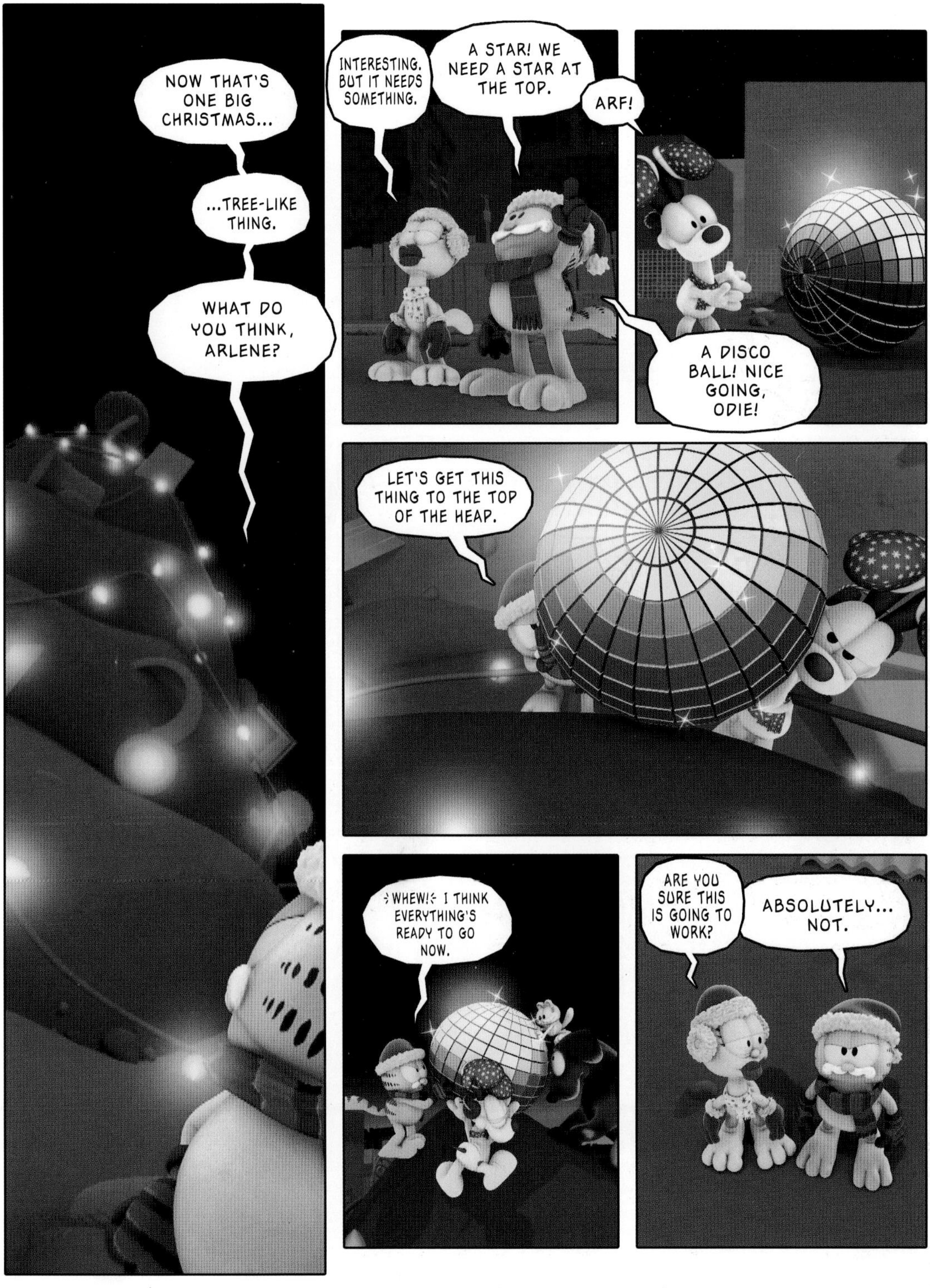
NOW THAT'S ONE BIG CHRISTMAS...
...TREE-LIKE THING.
WHAT DO YOU THINK, ARLENE?
INTERESTING. BUT IT NEEDS SOMETHING.
A STAR! WE NEED A STAR AT THE TOP.
ARF!
A DISCO BALL! NICE GOING, ODIE!
LET'S GET THIS THING TO THE TOP OF THE HEAP.
WHEW! I THINK EVERYTHING'S READY TO GO NOW.
ARE YOU SURE THIS IS GOING TO WORK?
ABSOLUTELY... NOT.

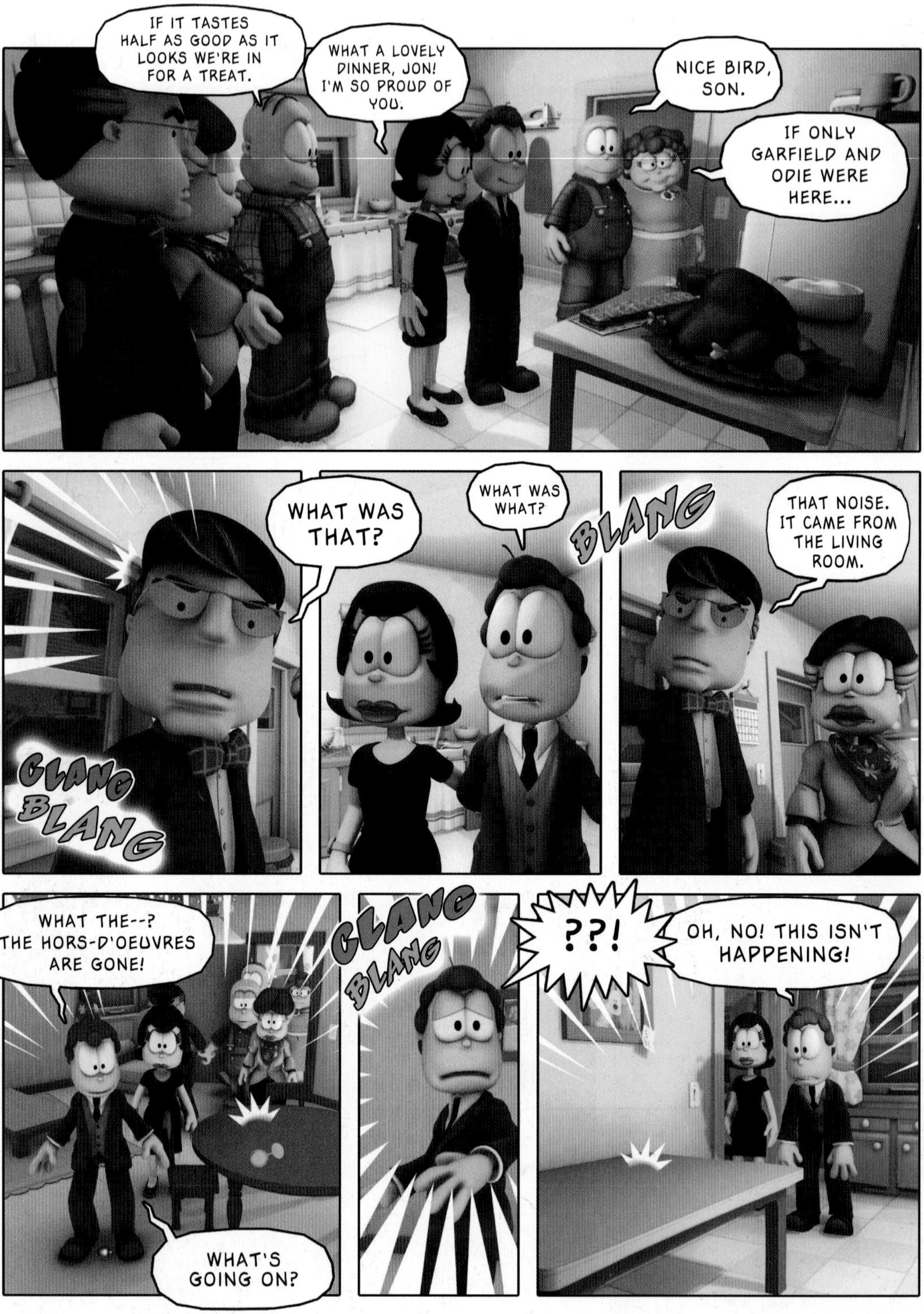
IF IT TASTES HALF AS GOOD AS IT LOOKS WE'RE IN FOR A TREAT.
WHAT A LOVELY DINNER, JON! I'M SO PROUD OF YOU.
NICE BIRD, SON.
IF ONLY GARFIELD AND ODIE WERE HERE...
WHAT WAS THAT?
CLANG
BLANG
WHAT WAS WHAT?
BLANG
THAT NOISE. IT CAME FROM THE LIVING ROOM.
WHAT THE--? THE HORS-D'OEUVRES ARE GONE!
WHAT'S GOING ON?
CLANG
BLANG
??!
OH, NO! THIS ISN'T HAPPENING!

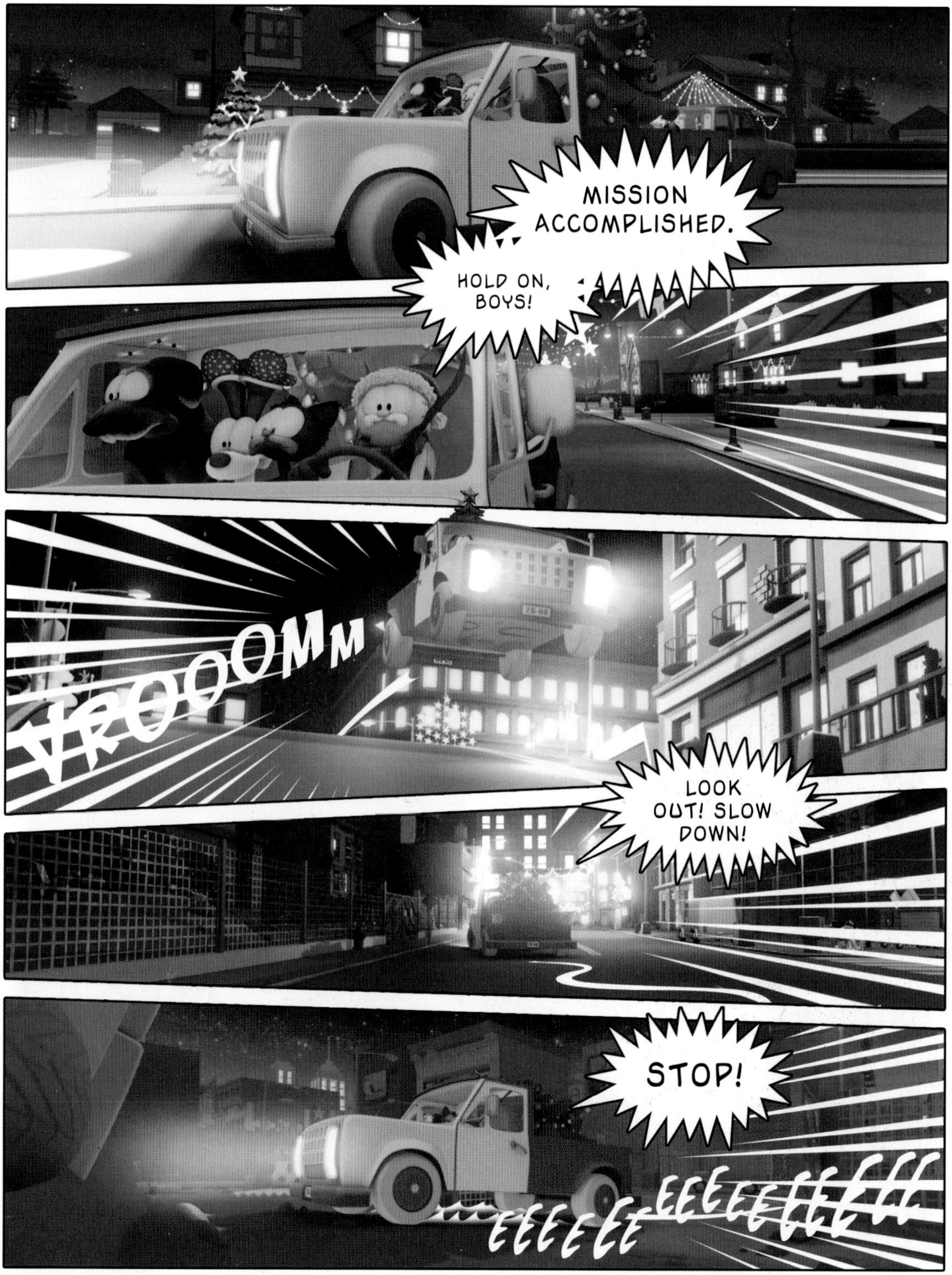
MISSION ACCOMPLISHED.
HOLD ON, BOYS!
AAAAAAA
VROOOMM
LOOK OUT! SLOW DOWN!
STOP!
EEEEEEEEEEEEEEEEEEEE

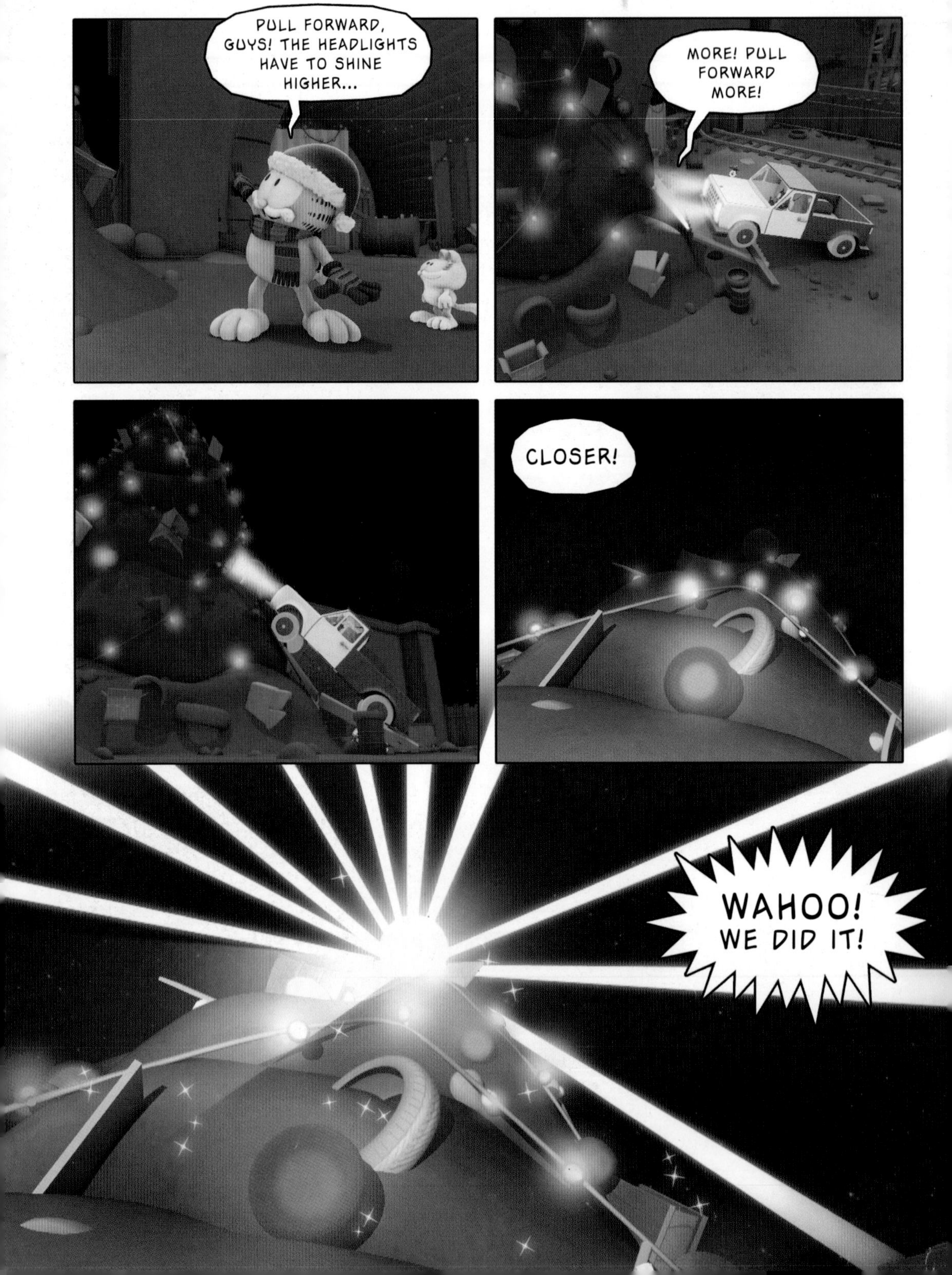
PULL FORWARD, GUYS! THE HEADLIGHTS HAVE TO SHINE HIGHER...
MORE! PULL FORWARD MORE!
CLOSER!
WAHOO! WE DID IT!

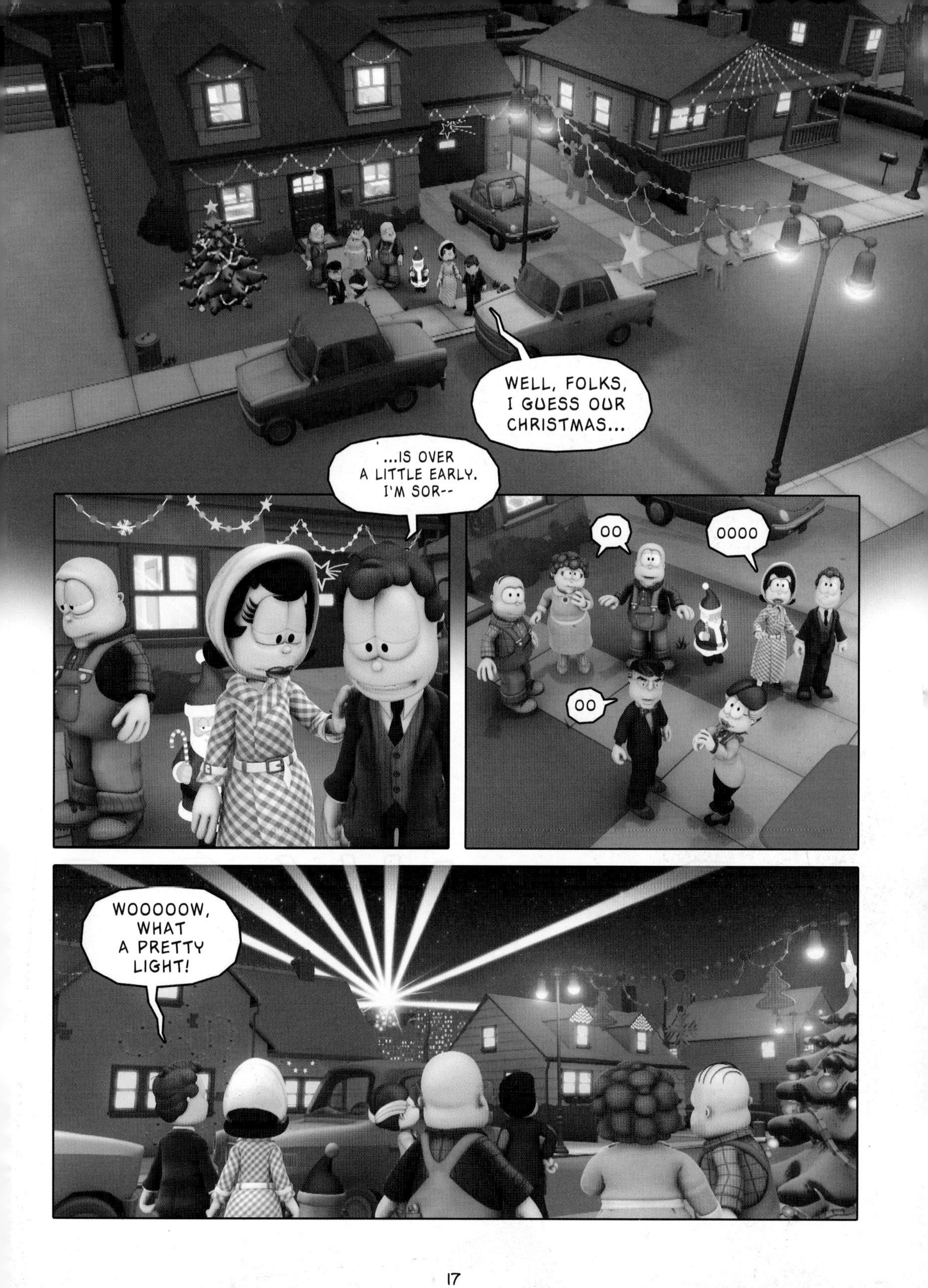
WELL, FOLKS, I GUESS OUR CHRISTMAS...
...IS OVER A LITTLE EARLY. I'M SOR--
OO
OOOO
OO
WOOOOOW, WHAT A PRETTY LIGHT!

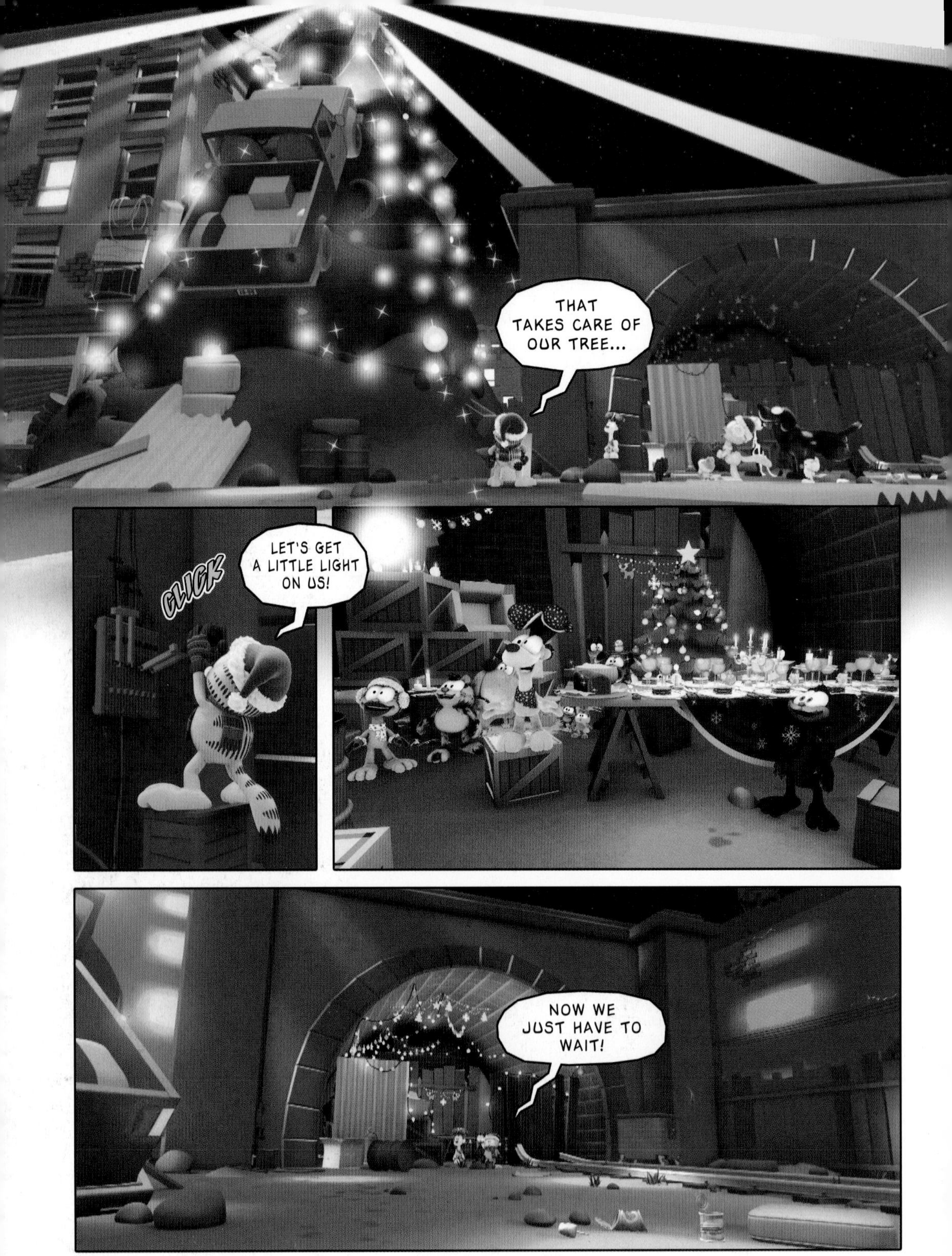
THAT TAKES CARE OF OUR TREE...
CLICK
LET'S GET A LITTLE LIGHT ON US!
NOW WE JUST HAVE TO WAIT!

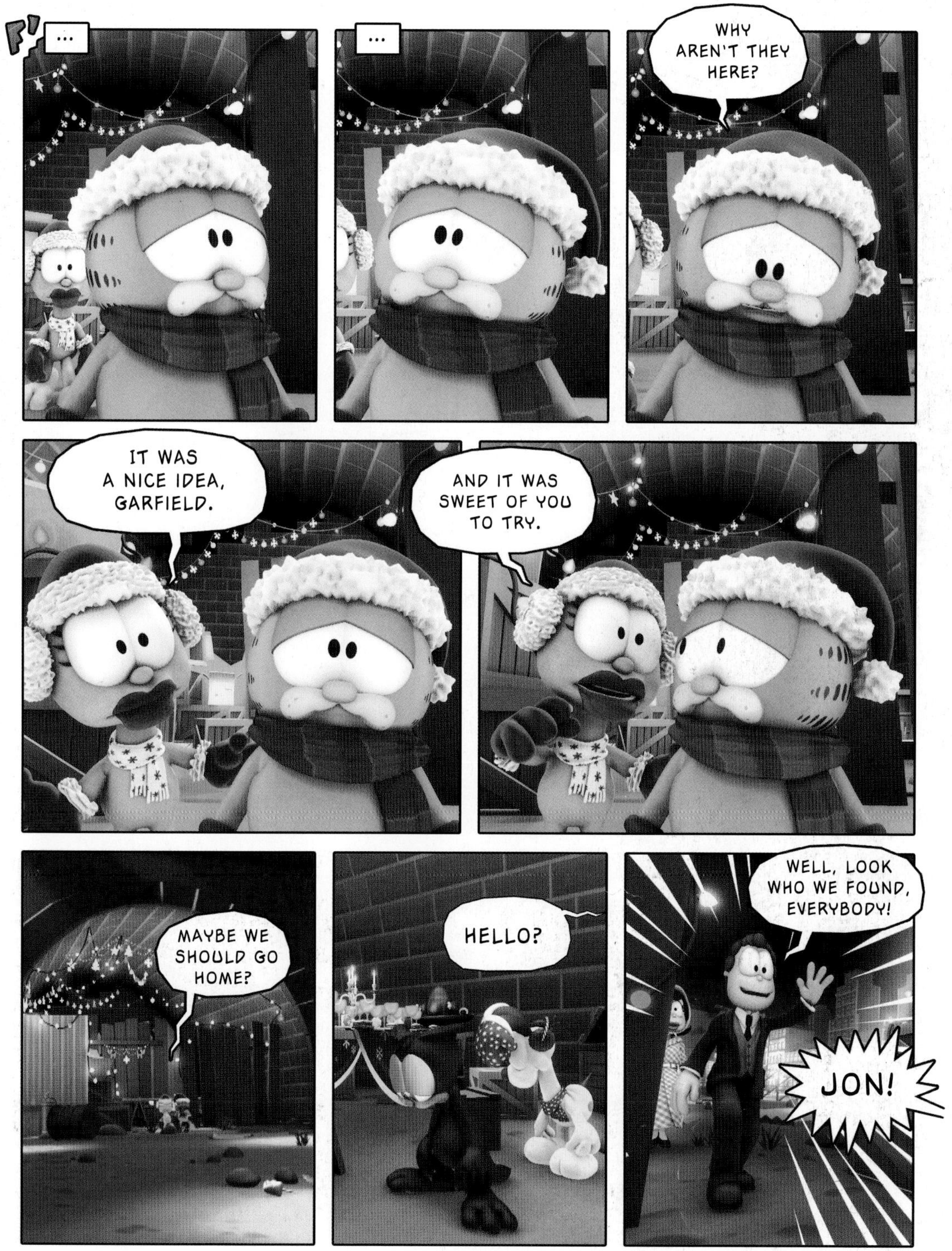

...
...
WHY AREN'T THEY HERE?
IT WAS A NICE IDEA, GARFIELD.
AND IT WAS SWEET OF YOU TO TRY.
MAYBE WE SHOULD GO HOME?
HELLO?
WELL, LOOK WHO WE FOUND, EVERYBODY!
JON!

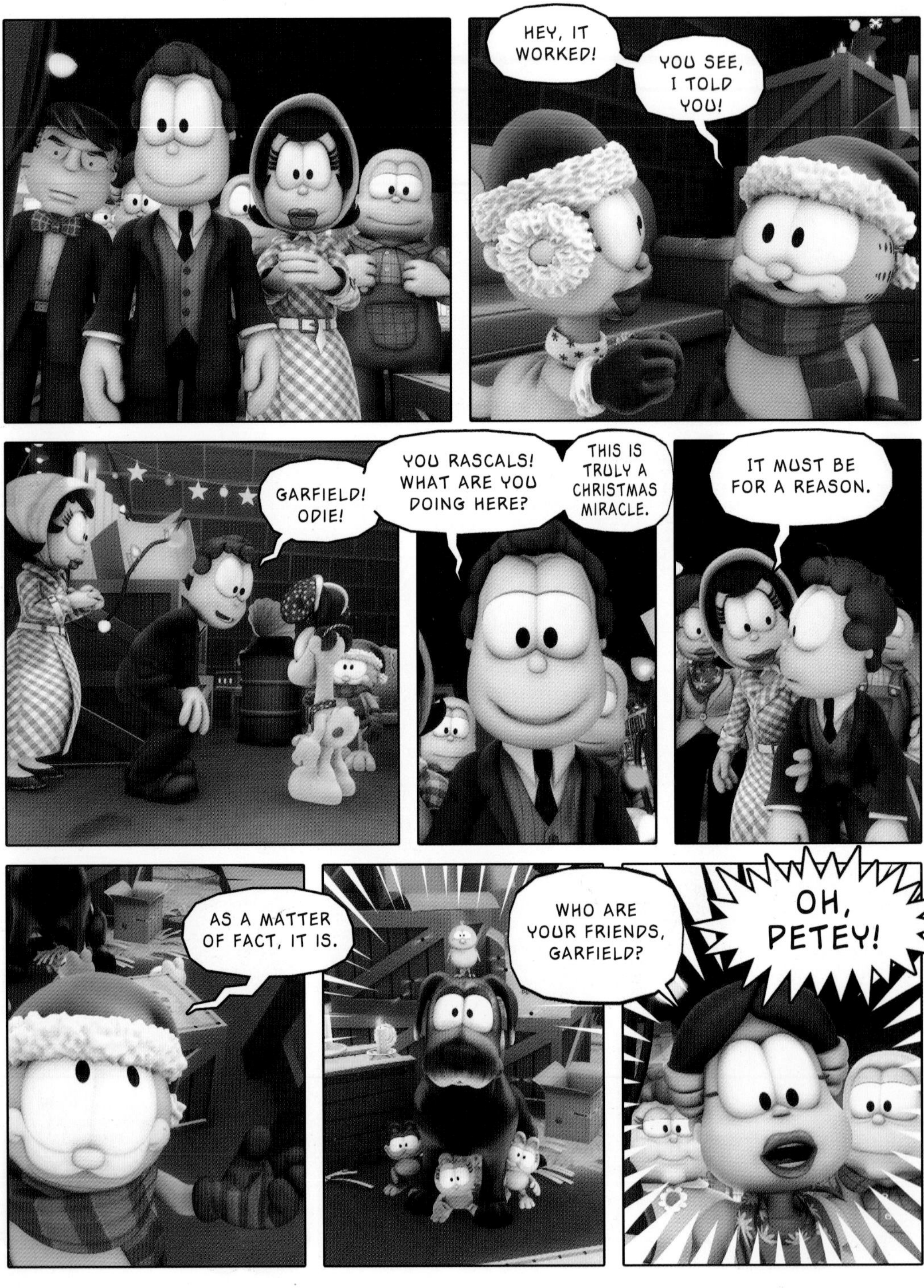
HEY, IT WORKED!
YOU SEE, I TOLD YOU!
GARFIELD! ODIE!
YOU RASCALS! WHAT ARE YOU DOING HERE?
THIS IS TRULY A CHRISTMAS MIRACLE.
IT MUST BE FOR A REASON.
AS A MATTER OF FACT, IT IS.
WHO ARE YOUR FRIENDS, GARFIELD?
OH, PETEY!

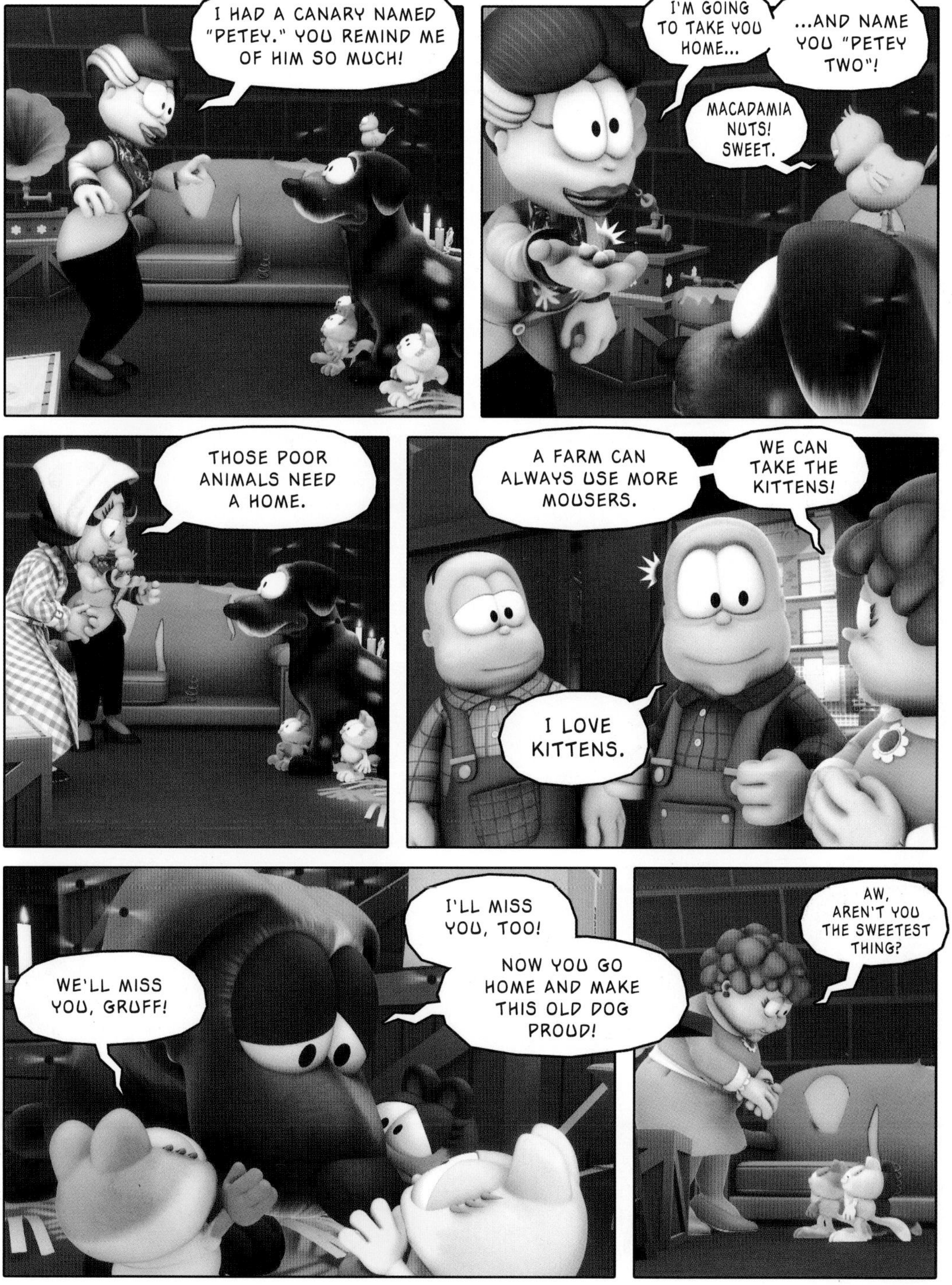
I HAD A CANARY NAMED "PETEY." YOU REMIND ME OF HIM SO MUCH!
I'M GOING TO TAKE YOU HOME...
...AND NAME YOU "PETEY TWO"!
MACADAMIA NUTS! SWEET.
THOSE POOR ANIMALS NEED A HOME.
A FARM CAN ALWAYS USE MORE MOUSERS.
WE CAN TAKE THE KITTENS!
I LOVE KITTENS.
WE'LL MISS YOU, GRUFF!
I'LL MISS YOU, TOO!
NOW YOU GO HOME AND MAKE THIS OLD DOG PROUD!
AW, AREN'T YOU THE SWEETEST THING?

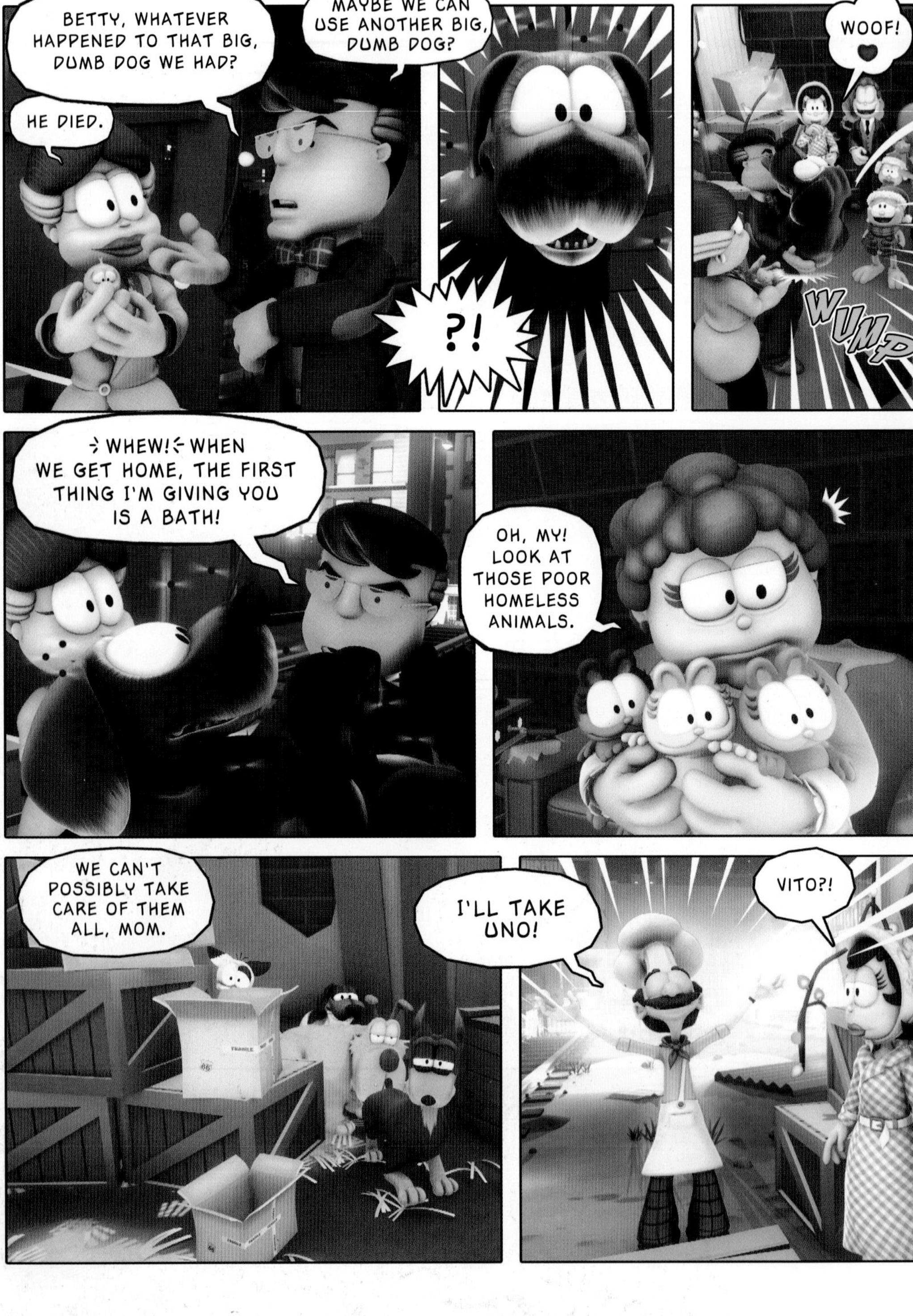

BETTY, WHATEVER HAPPENED TO THAT BIG, DUMB DOG WE HAD?
HE DIED.
MAYBE WE CAN USE ANOTHER BIG, DUMB DOG?
?!
WOOF!
WUMP
-WHEW!- WHEN WE GET HOME, THE FIRST THING I'M GIVING YOU IS A BATH!
OH, MY! LOOK AT THOSE POOR HOMELESS ANIMALS.
WE CAN'T POSSIBLY TAKE CARE OF THEM ALL, MOM.
I'LL TAKE UNO!
VITO?!

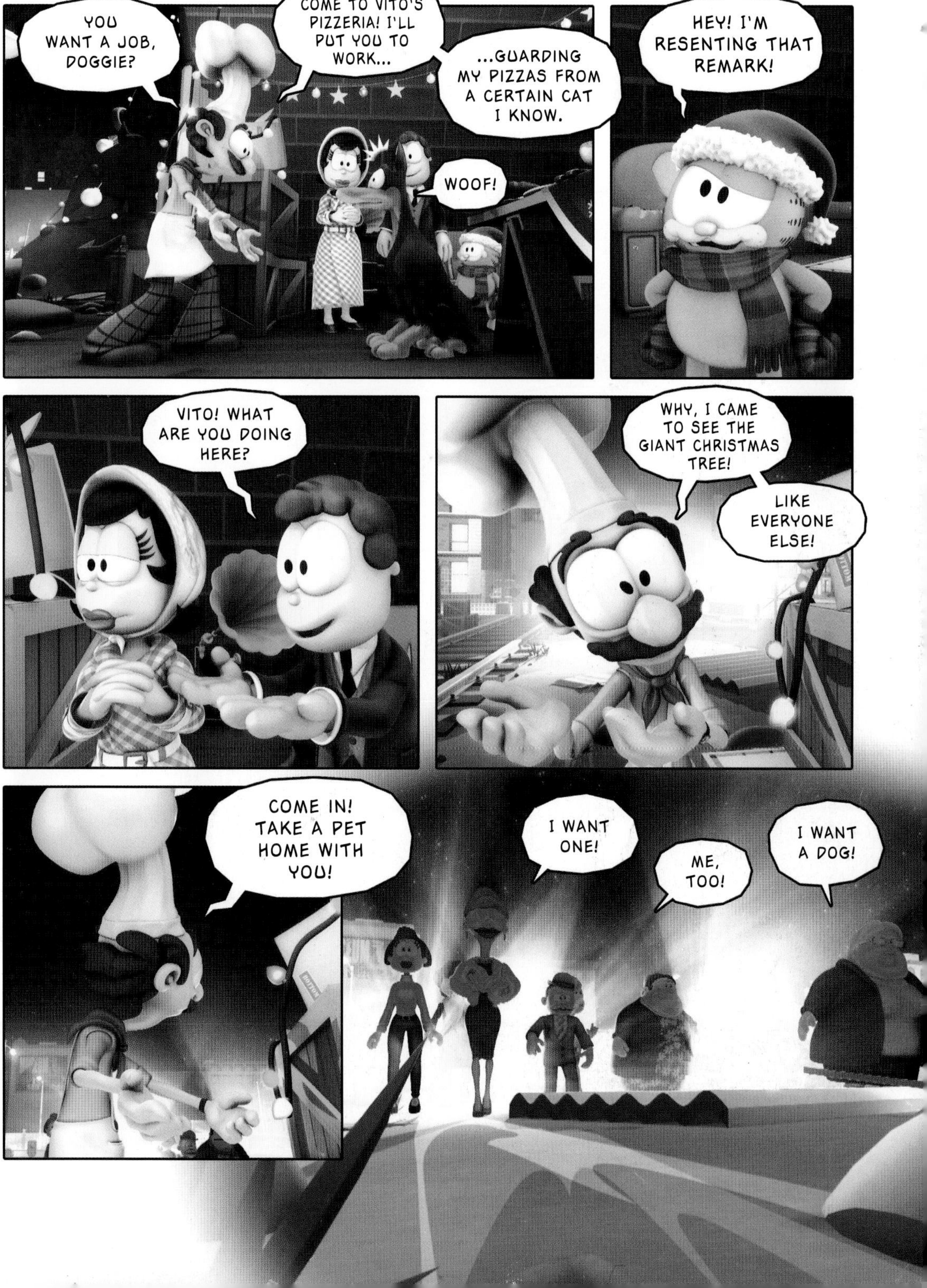
YOU WANT A JOB, DOGGIE?
COME TO VITO'S PIZZERIA! I'LL PUT YOU TO WORK...
...GUARDING MY PIZZAS FROM A CERTAIN CAT I KNOW.
WOOF!
HEY! I'M RESENTING THAT REMARK!
VITO! WHAT ARE YOU DOING HERE?
WHY, I CAME TO SEE THE GIANT CHRISTMAS TREE!
LIKE EVERYONE ELSE!
COME IN! TAKE A PET HOME WITH YOU!
I WANT ONE!
ME, TOO!
I WANT A DOG!

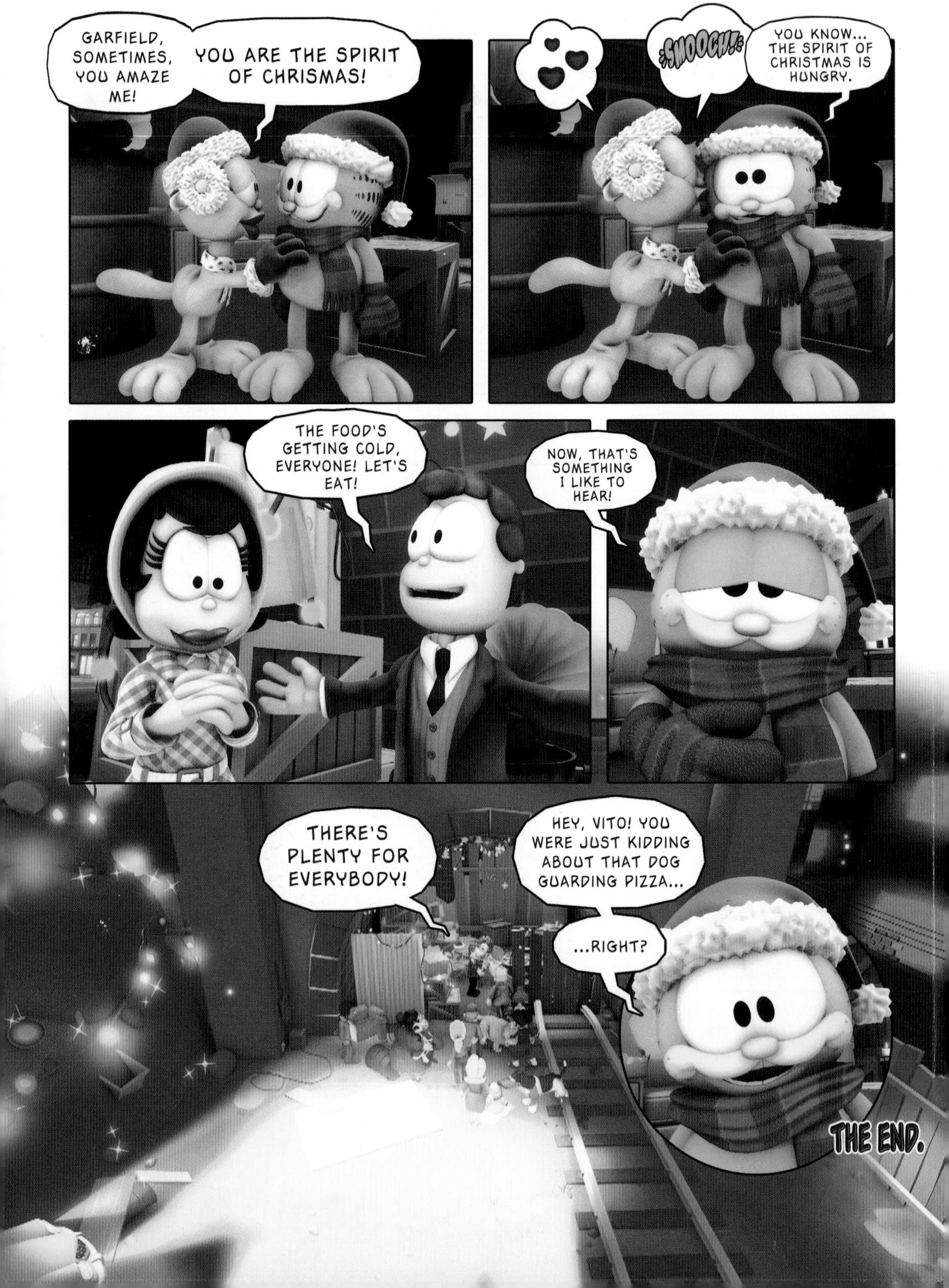
GARFIELD, SOMETIMES, YOU AMAZE ME!
YOU ARE THE SPIRIT OF CHRISMAS!
SMOOCH!
YOU KNOW... THE SPIRIT OF CHRISTMAS IS HUNGRY.
THE FOOD'S GETTING COLD, EVERYONE! LET'S EAT!
NOW, THAT'S SOMETHING I LIKE TO HEAR!
THERE'S PLENTY FOR EVERYBODY!
HEY, VITO! YOU WERE JUST KIDDING ABOUT THAT DOG GUARDING PIZZA...
...RIGHT?
THE END.

WATCH OUT FOR PAPERCUTZ™

Welcome to the seasonally sweet, sentimental, and somewhat spooky seventh GARFIELD & Co graphic novel from Papercutz. We're the folks dedicated to publishing great graphic novels for all ages. I'm your Scrooge-like Editor-in-Chief, Jim Salicrup. While our favorite orange fat cat does discover the Christmas spirit in "Home for the Holidays," he doesn't actually meet a real spirit until our second story "The Haunted House."

Speaking of ol' Scrooge, here's a quick peek at a page written by Rodolphe and illustrated by Estelle Meyrand adapting "A Christmas Carol" by Charles Dickens from CLASSICS ILLUSTRATED DELUXE #9, featuring both Christams and a real spirit:

Merry Christmas to you!
Grrrr...
Scrooge and Marley's, I believe. Have I the pleasure of addressing Mr. Scrooge, or Mr. Marley?
Mr. Marley has been dead these seven years.
What do you want?
We're soliciting the liberality of each so the destitute may have a roof this night.
A roof?
Are there no prisons? Prisons have roofs, do they not?
And the workhouses? Are they still in operation?
Of course! But at this time of the year, a small coin may allow them to buy some meat and means of warmth...

If you like what you see here, be sure to pick up CLASSICS ILLUSTRATED DELUXE #9 SCROOGE "A Christmas Carol" & "A Remembrance of Mugby." You're probably seen a gazillion adaptations of "A Christmas Carol," but are you familiar with another Christmas story by Charles Dickens entitled "Mugby Junction"? I wasn't, and really enjoyed the comics adaptation, also by Rodolphe and Estelle Meyrand.

But back to good ol' GARFIELD & Co. We wanted to mention that although Jon Arbuckle struggles to dream up an idea for a new comicbook, our friends over at kaboom! came up with a great idea: GARFIELD comics! And writing the all-new GARFIELD comicbook is none other than Mark Evanier, who happens to be the Supervising Producer of The Garfield Show. "I have no idea what a Supervising Producer is supposed to do but I write and story-edit and direct the voices," Mark explains on his popular blog, www.newsfromme.com. Look for the new GARFIELD comics wherever comics are sold.

And don't forget about us! We'll be back soon with GARFIELD & Co #8 "Secret Agent X"! For more information on GARFIELD & Co graphic novels, and news on what else we're up to at Papercutz, visit our spiffy new website at www.papercutz.com.! Until next time, enjoy the upcoming holidays (however you choose to do so) and have a Happy New Year!

Jim

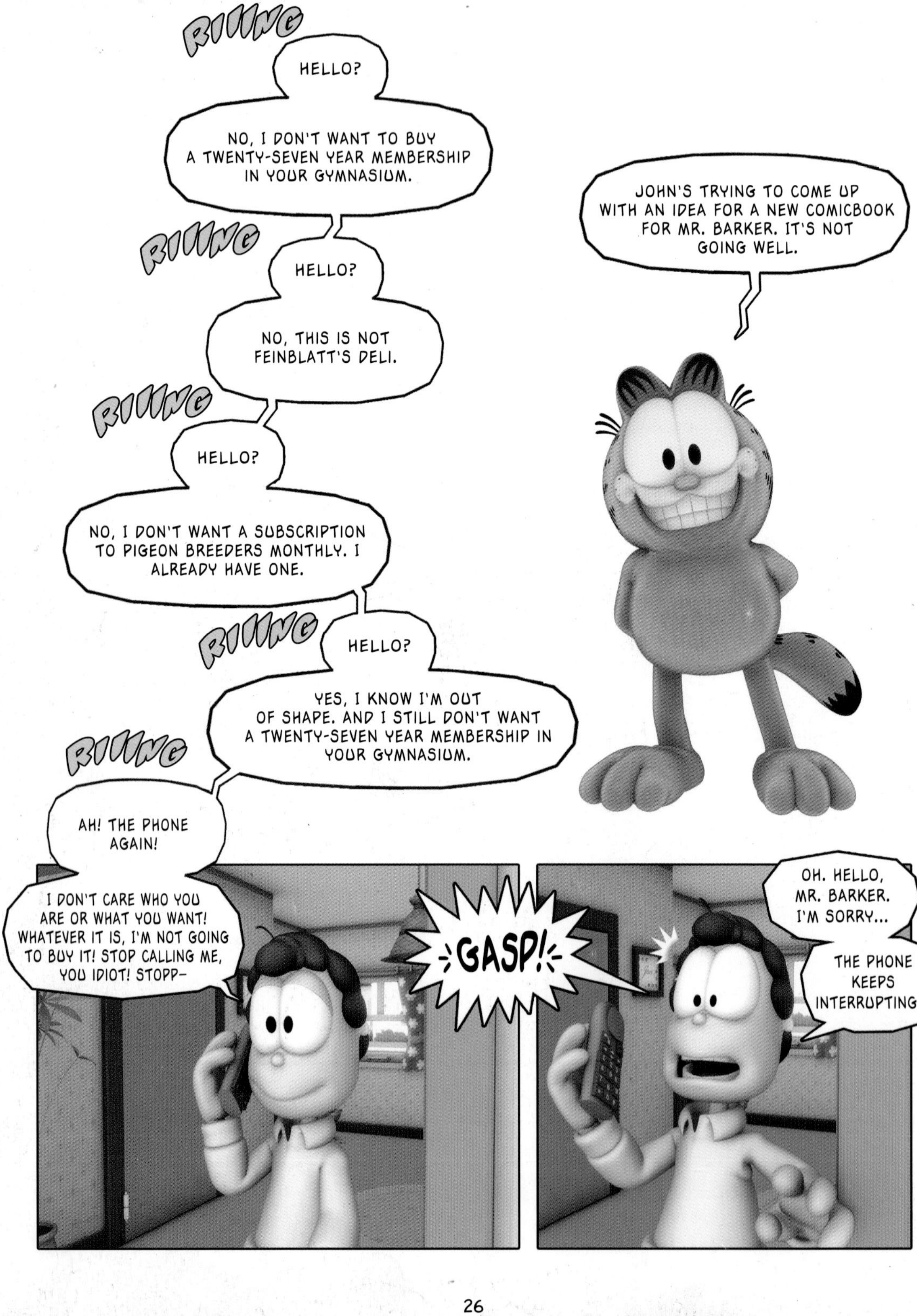
JOHN'S TRYING TO COME UP WITH AN IDEA FOR A NEW COMICBOOK FOR MR. BARKER. IT'S NOT GOING WELL.
RIIING
HELLO?
NO, I DON'T WANT TO BUY A TWENTY-SEVEN YEAR MEMBERSHIP IN YOUR GYMNASIUM.
RIIING
HELLO?
NO, THIS IS NOT FEINBLATT'S DELI.
RIIING
HELLO?
NO, I DON'T WANT A SUBSCRIPTION TO PIGEON BREEDERS MONTHLY. I ALREADY HAVE ONE.
RIIING
HELLO?
YES, I KNOW I'M OUT OF SHAPE. AND I STILL DON'T WANT A TWENTY-SEVEN YEAR MEMBERSHIP IN YOUR GYMNASIUM.
RIIING
AH! THE PHONE AGAIN!
I DON'T CARE WHO YOU ARE OR WHAT YOU WANT! WHATEVER IT IS, I'M NOT GOING TO BUY IT! STOP CALLING ME, YOU IDIOT! STOPP–
GASP!
OH. HELLO, MR. BARKER. I'M SORRY...
THE PHONE KEEPS INTERRUPTING...

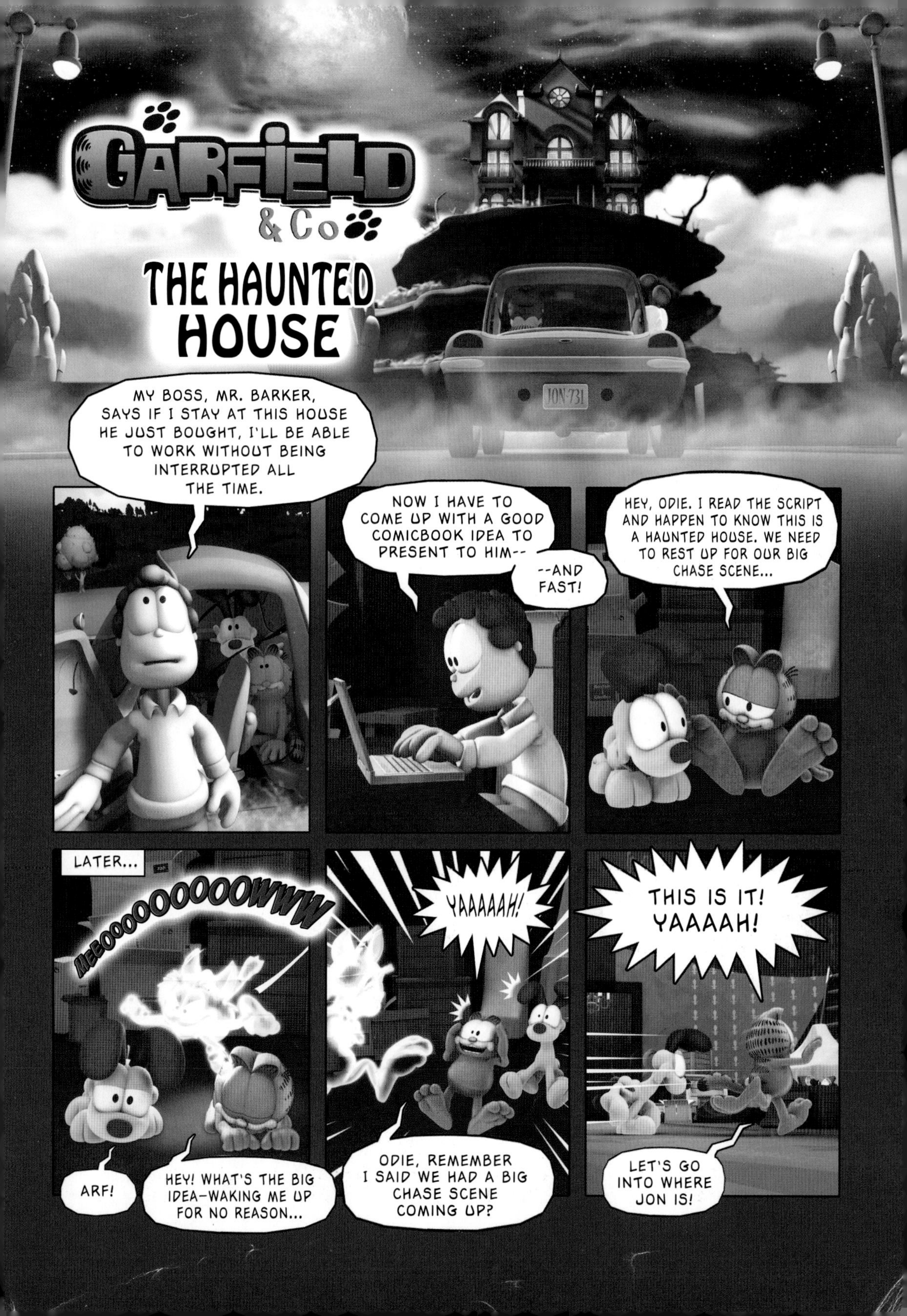
GARFIELD
& Co
THE HAUNTED HOUSE
JON-731
MY BOSS, MR. BARKER, SAYS IF I STAY AT THIS HOUSE HE JUST BOUGHT, I'LL BE ABLE TO WORK WITHOUT BEING INTERRUPTED ALL THE TIME.
NOW I HAVE TO COME UP WITH A GOOD COMICBOOK IDEA TO PRESENT TO HIM--
--AND FAST!
HEY, ODIE. I READ THE SCRIPT AND HAPPEN TO KNOW THIS IS A HAUNTED HOUSE. WE NEED TO REST UP FOR OUR BIG CHASE SCENE...
LATER...
MEEOOOOOOOOOOWWW
ARF!
HEY! WHAT'S THE BIG IDEA—WAKING ME UP FOR NO REASON...
YAAAAAH!
ODIE, REMEMBER I SAID WE HAD A BIG CHASE SCENE COMING UP?
THIS IS IT! YAAAAH!
LET'S GO INTO WHERE JON IS!

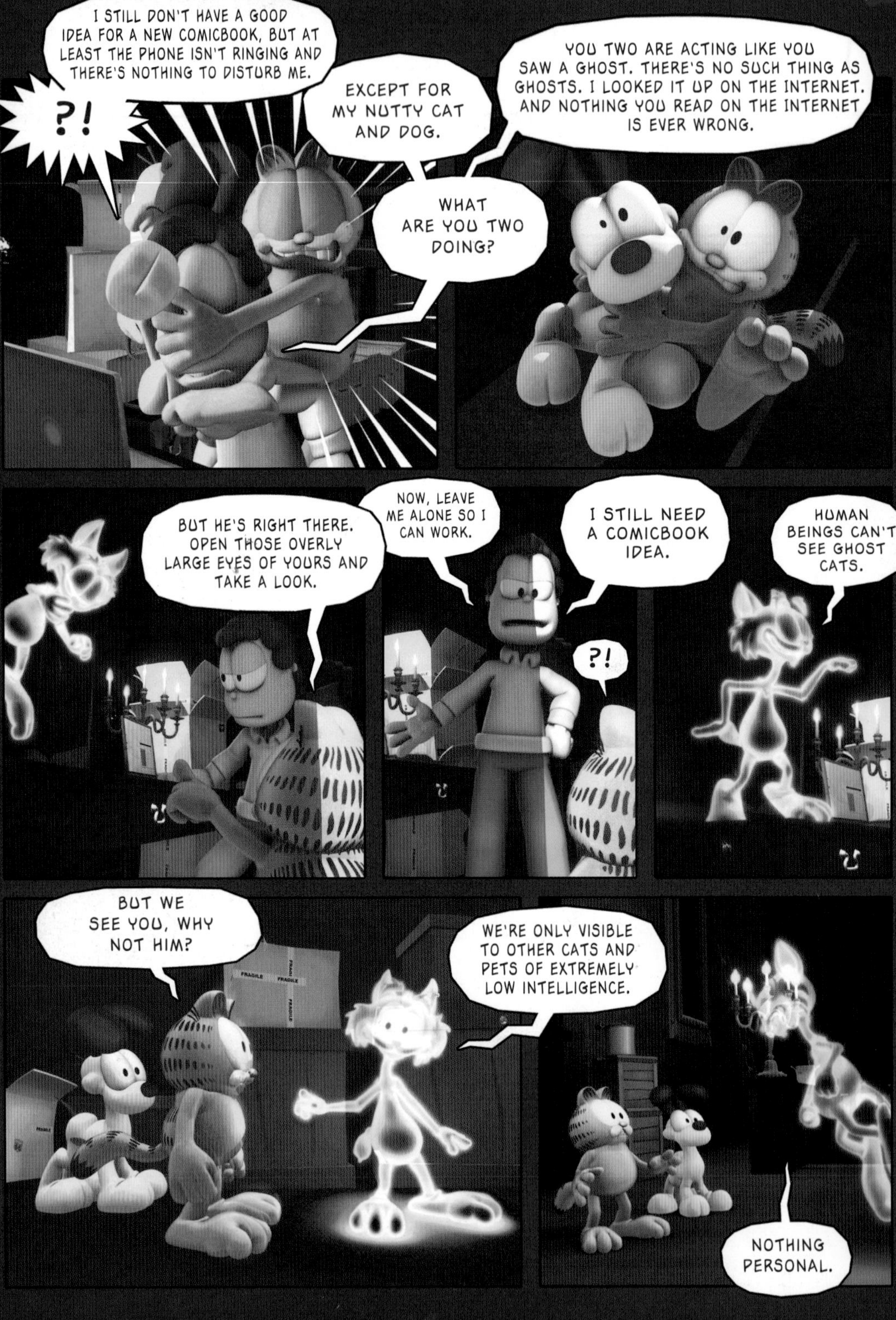

I STILL DON'T HAVE A GOOD IDEA FOR A NEW COMICBOOK, BUT AT LEAST THE PHONE ISN'T RINGING AND THERE'S NOTHING TO DISTURB ME.
?!
EXCEPT FOR MY NUTTY CAT AND DOG.
WHAT ARE YOU TWO DOING?
YOU TWO ARE ACTING LIKE YOU SAW A GHOST. THERE'S NO SUCH THING AS GHOSTS. I LOOKED IT UP ON THE INTERNET. AND NOTHING YOU READ ON THE INTERNET IS EVER WRONG.
BUT HE'S RIGHT THERE. OPEN THOSE OVERLY LARGE EYES OF YOURS AND TAKE A LOOK.
NOW, LEAVE ME ALONE SO I CAN WORK.
I STILL NEED A COMICBOOK IDEA.
?!
HUMAN BEINGS CAN'T SEE GHOST CATS.
BUT WE SEE YOU, WHY NOT HIM?
WE'RE ONLY VISIBLE TO OTHER CATS AND PETS OF EXTREMELY LOW INTELLIGENCE.
NOTHING PERSONAL.

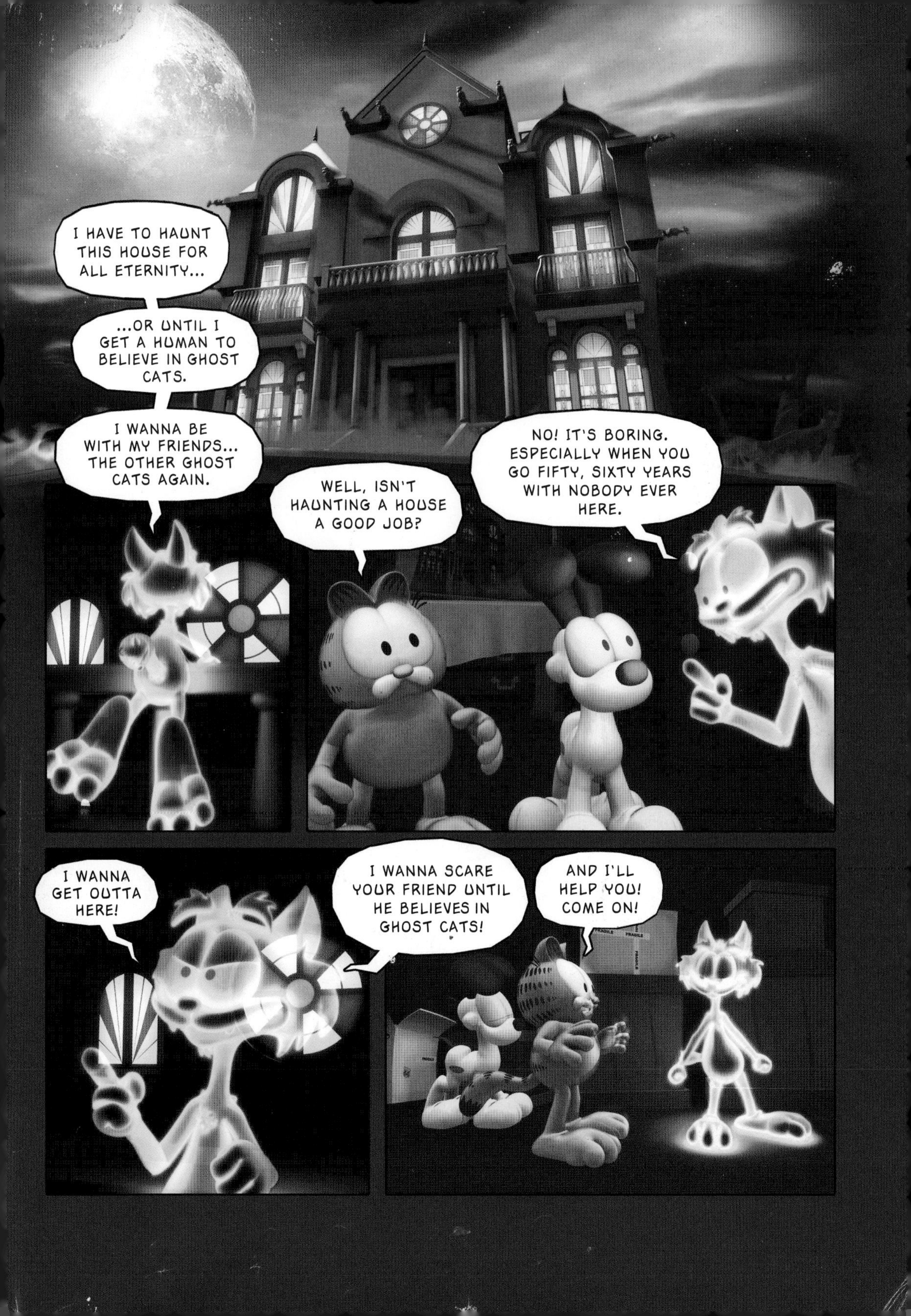
I HAVE TO HAUNT THIS HOUSE FOR ALL ETERNITY...
...OR UNTIL I GET A HUMAN TO BELIEVE IN GHOST CATS.
I WANNA BE WITH MY FRIENDS... THE OTHER GHOST CATS AGAIN.
WELL, ISN'T HAUNTING A HOUSE A GOOD JOB?
NO! IT'S BORING. ESPECIALLY WHEN YOU GO FIFTY, SIXTY YEARS WITH NOBODY EVER HERE.
I WANNA GET OUTTA HERE!
I WANNA SCARE YOUR FRIEND UNTIL HE BELIEVES IN GHOST CATS!
AND I'LL HELP YOU! COME ON!

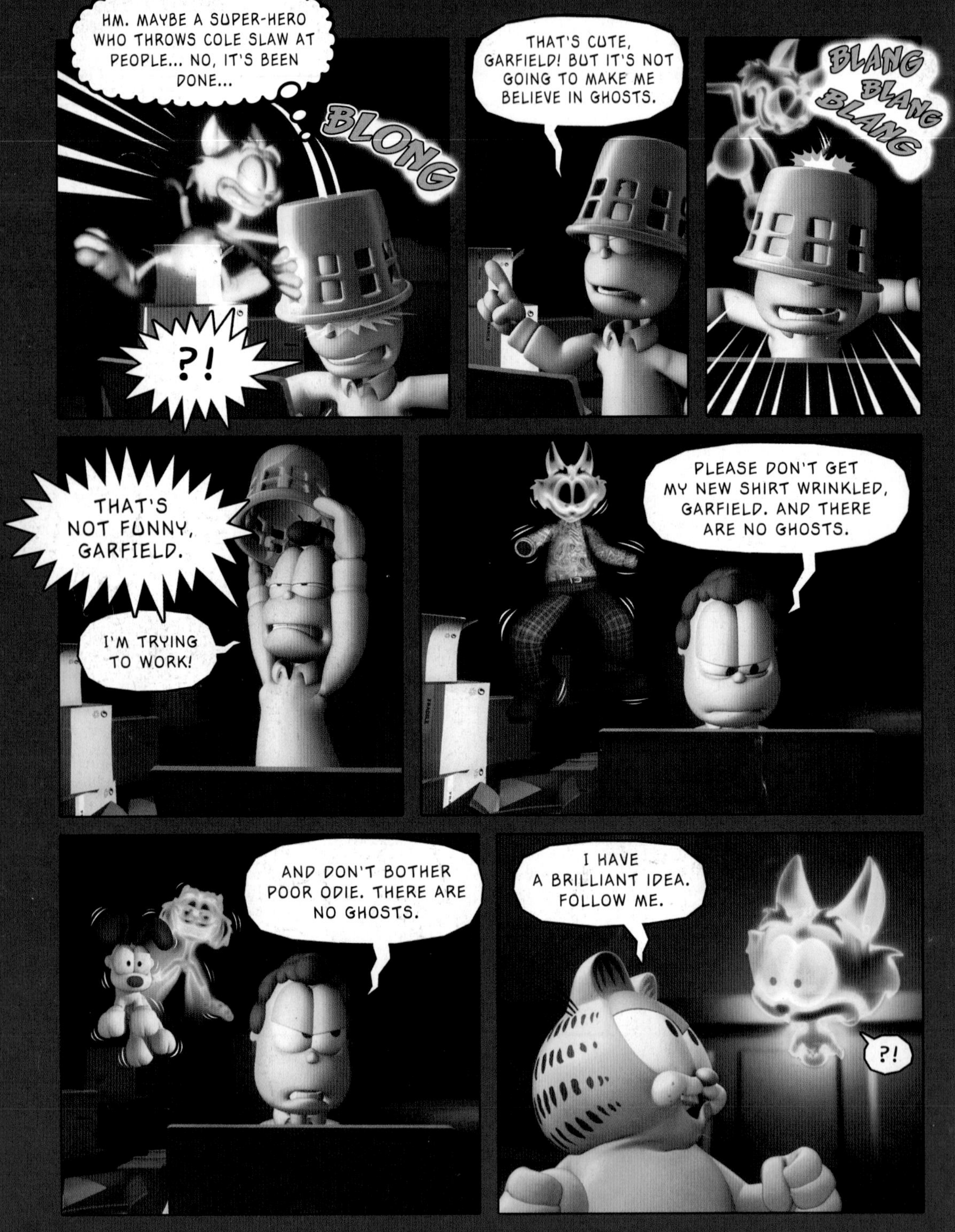
HM. MAYBE A SUPER-HERO WHO THROWS COLE SLAW AT PEOPLE... NO, IT'S BEEN DONE...
BLONG
?!
THAT'S CUTE, GARFIELD! BUT IT'S NOT GOING TO MAKE ME BELIEVE IN GHOSTS.
BLANG BLANG BLANG
THAT'S NOT FUNNY, GARFIELD.
I'M TRYING TO WORK!
PLEASE DON'T GET MY NEW SHIRT WRINKLED, GARFIELD. AND THERE ARE NO GHOSTS.
AND DON'T BOTHER POOR ODIE. THERE ARE NO GHOSTS.
I HAVE A BRILLIANT IDEA. FOLLOW ME.
?!

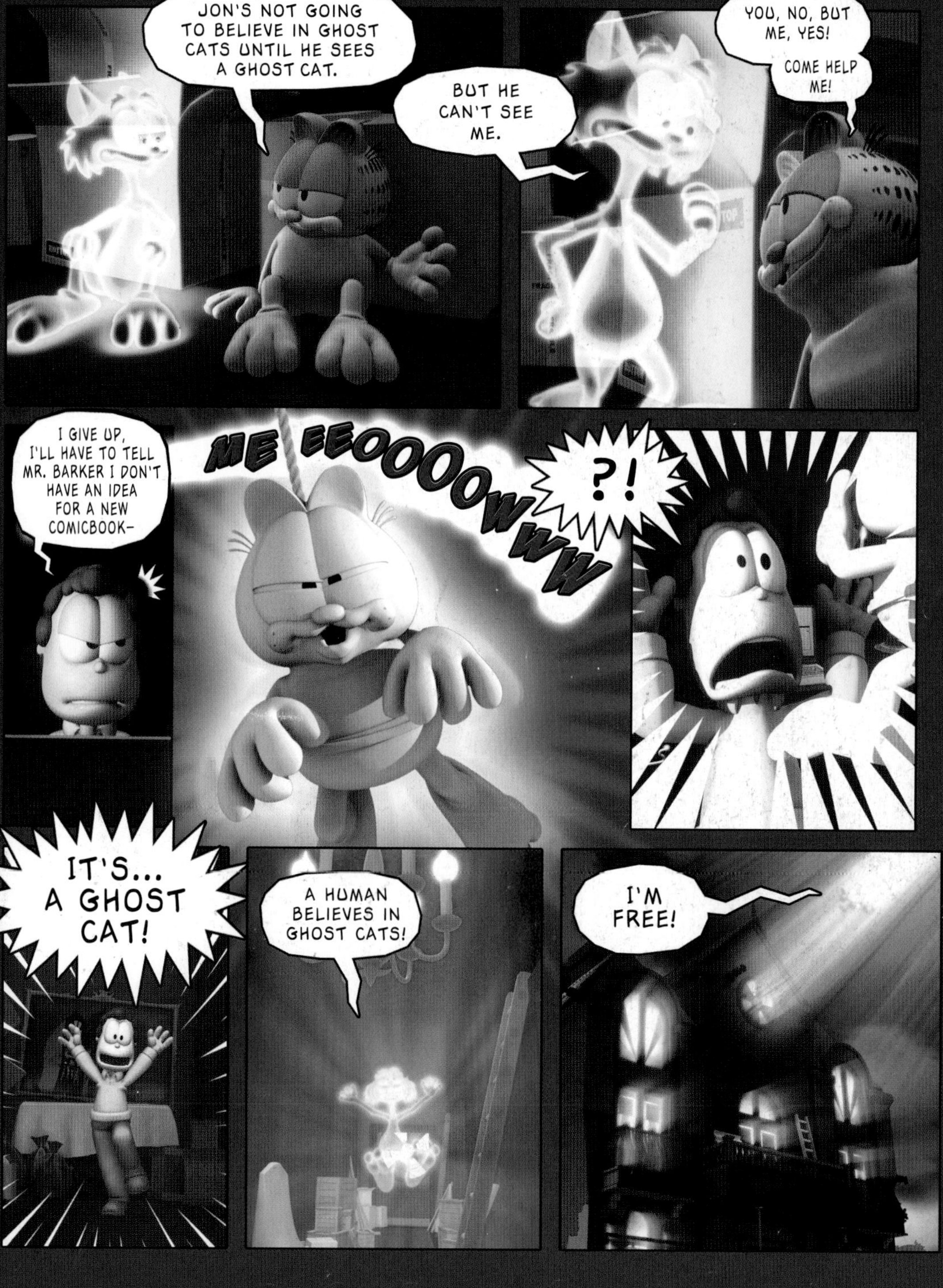
JON'S NOT GOING TO BELIEVE IN GHOST CATS UNTIL HE SEES A GHOST CAT.
BUT HE CAN'T SEE ME.
YOU, NO, BUT ME, YES!
COME HELP ME!
I GIVE UP, I'LL HAVE TO TELL MR. BARKER I DON'T HAVE AN IDEA FOR A NEW COMICBOOK–
ME EEOOOOOWWWW
?!
IT'S... A GHOST CAT!
A HUMAN BELIEVES IN GHOST CATS!
I'M FREE!

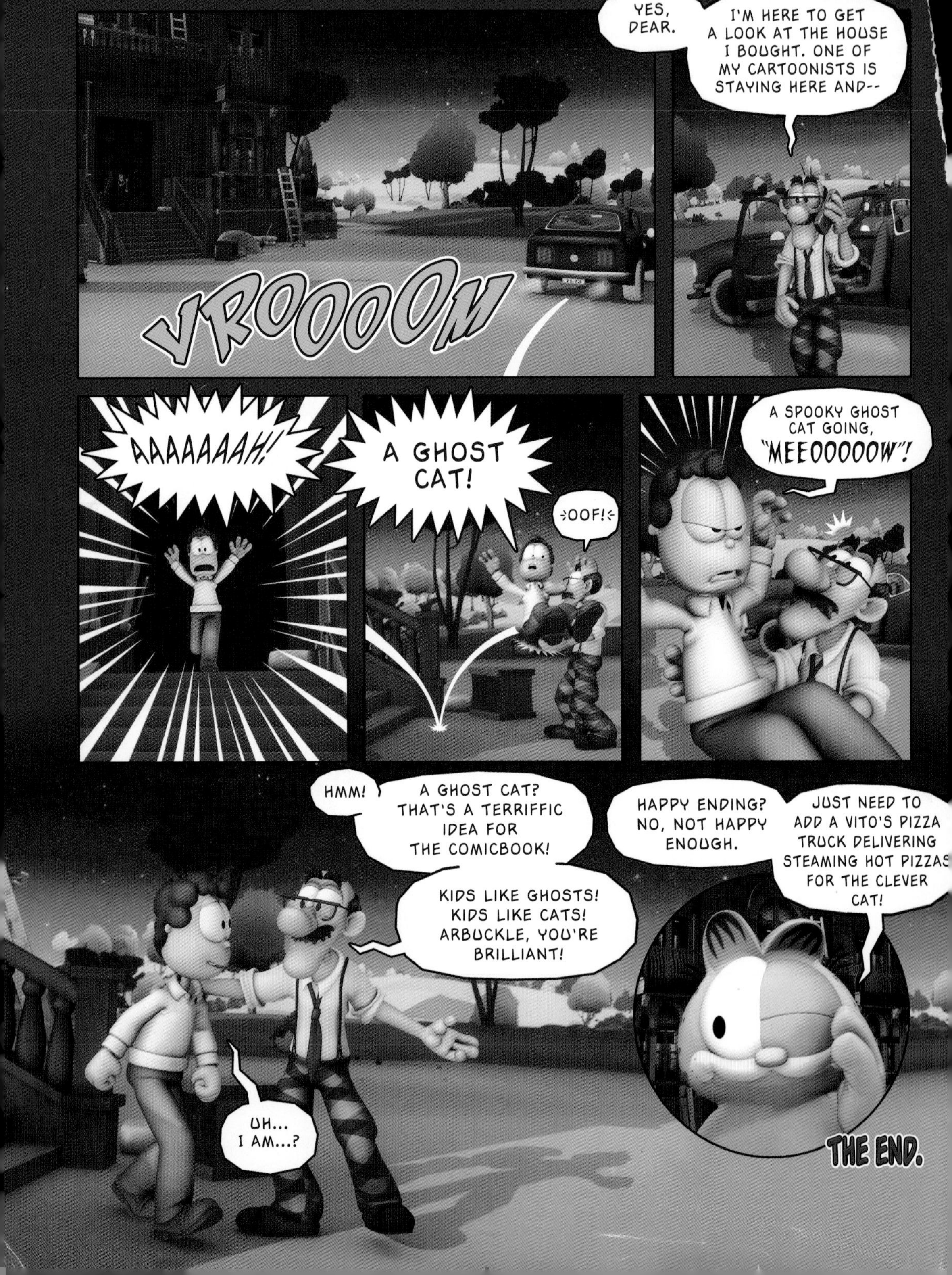
VROOOOOM
YES, DEAR.
I'M HERE TO GET A LOOK AT THE HOUSE I BOUGHT. ONE OF MY CARTOONISTS IS STAYING HERE AND--
AAAAAAAH!
A GHOST CAT!
OOF!
A SPOOKY GHOST CAT GOING, "MEEOOOOOW"!
HMM!
A GHOST CAT? THAT'S A TERRIFFIC IDEA FOR THE COMICBOOK!
KIDS LIKE GHOSTS! KIDS LIKE CATS! ARBUCKLE, YOU'RE BRILLIANT!
UH... I AM...?
HAPPY ENDING? NO, NOT HAPPY ENOUGH.
JUST NEED TO ADD A VITO'S PIZZA TRUCK DELIVERING STEAMING HOT PIZZAS FOR THE CLEVER CAT!
THE END.